D1488428

ONE-TIME DOG MARKET AT BUDA

ONE-TIME DOG MARKET AT BUDA

and Other Hungarian Folktales

Translated and retold by Irma Molnár
Illustrations by Georgeta-Elena Eneşel

Linnet Books
North Haven, Connecticut

© 2001 Irma Molnár. All rights reserved.
First published 2001 as a Linnet Book,
an imprint of The Shoe String Press, Inc.,
2 Linsley Street, North Haven, Connecticut 06473.
www.shoestringpress.com

Library of Congress Cataloging-in-Publication Data

Molnár, Irma, 1940–
One-time dog market at Buda and other Hungarian folktales / translated
and retold by Irma Molnár ; illustrations by Georgeta-Elena Eneşel.
    p. cm.
Includes bibliographical references.
    Summary: Presents twenty-three Hungarian folktales, featuring historical
figures such as King Matthias, legends about the founding of Hungary
and the Mongol raids, Turkish tales, Gypsy stories, and tales that reflect
Hungary's geographical position as a meeting and fighting place in east-
central Europe.
    ISBN 0-208-02505-7 (library binding : alk. paper)
    1. Tales—Hungary [1. Folklore—Hungary.] I. Molnár, Irma. II. Eneşel,
Georgeta-Elena, ill.

PZ8.1.O556 2001
398.2'09439—dc21

                                                                2001038836

The paper in this publication meets the minimum requirements of
American National Standard for Information Sciences—Permanence of
Paper for Printed Library Materials,
                    ANSI-Z39.1984∞

Designed by Dutton and Sherman

Printed in the United States of America

FOR
VIRGINIA L. MCFARLAND
OF OKLAHOMA CITY, OKLAHOMA

CONTENTS

ACKNOWLEDGMENTS

The following friends have provided me with resource materials for the preparation of this book: Megyesy Jenö, Budapest and Oklahoma City, himself the author of numerous books in Hungarian; Molnár Adél, Budapest, graduate of the University of Budapest with a major in Hungarian language and literature; and Szilágyi Mária, librarian, the University of Chicago Library, Szatmáry Lajos (Louis) Family Collection of Hungarica.

The computer skills of my friend, James McFarland, Oklahoma City, turned quill and inkpot into a laser-printed manuscript. Dolly Dearner, Ph.D., and her husband, James, encouraged my writing efforts every step of the way.

Finally, Diantha C. Thorpe, owner and editor of The Shoe String Press, Inc., took my rough-sawn timbers, planed and sanded them, and made them a thing of beauty. The fruition of my years of work is owing to her patient guidance through the labyrinth called publishing.

INTRODUCTION

The title of this volume could easily have been *Hungarian Folktales, a Sampler.* Its twenty-three stories do not even scrape the surface of the material that has been collected. So far the number of recorded Hungarian folktales is more than ten thousand.

This vast array of tales has been classified by Dr. Berze Nagy János (1879–1946) in 612 tale types. His life work, the *Magyar Népmesetipusok (Hungarian Folktale Types),* reveals the distinctive features of Hungarian tales that distinguish them from the stories of other cultures. Most Hungarian oral tales begin with entertaining rigmarole that leads the listener into a fantasy world, such as this opening: "Once upon a time, beyond the seven seas and even farther, where the short-tailed piglet roots." Hungarian story endings are also specific, such as these four: "Here is the end, run away with it"; "They got seated into a nutshell and descended on the Küküllő River; tomorrow they will be your guests"; "They are still alive if they have not died";

and "He vanished into thin air, and no trace was ever found of him."

Sandwiched between is the stuff of the tale itself, and what most tales have in common is a nimble kind of cleverness. Wily kings match wits with equally clever peasants; students fool kings but are fooled by princesses; greedy folk are prey to smarter scoundrels or the simple straightforwardness of the poor. Lessons are taught to those who need them, not through moral precept but by having the tables turned, and logic is as often as not a by-product of how words are used. Most of the time the triumph belongs to the one who is not only clever, but also good-hearted.

The cradle of these folktales is in East-Central Europe, especially in the basin of the Carpathian Mountains, though some of them might have had their origin in the ancient homeland (Ural-Altaic region) of the Huns. Heroic tales, fun tales about fools, and some magic and fairy tales were already known before the Hungarian Conquest of the ninth century. Because Hungary is situated on a plain near the geographic center of Europe, it has been the meeting ground or battleground of many peoples, who brought their own folktales with them. These, too, have become part of the Hungarian story-bag.

Eleven hundred years ago, as one of the late waves in the Great Migrations, the Hungarian tribal alliance led by Prince Árpád arrived in the Carpathian Basin from beyond the Ural Mountains. Its members were Magyars, who spoke a language that was essentially Finno-Ugric. After bold military raids, which long kept Europe in fear, these people settled down on

East-Central European soil. Here they were able to found a national state which has endured to this very day.

In order to become a part of Europe, the Hungarians adopted western Christianity under Prince Vajk, who received the name Stephen on becoming a Christian. On December 25, 1000, he was crowned Hungary's first king with a crown sent by Pope Sylvester II. This crown was not simply an embodiment of royal power, but was also the symbol of general political authority, of legitimacy of rule. The Holy Crown remained in Hungary until World War II, when it was taken to the United States for safekeeping. Former president Jimmy Carter (1977–1981) was personally responsible for its return.

King Stephen's reign extended from 1000 to 1038. In the founding of the state, his leadership was basic to its success. Some sources describe him as a pious soul, but there was hardly a Hungarian king who was more iron-handed than he. For his role in Christianizing Hungary, he was raised by Rome to the rank of saint on August 20, 1083, as Saint Stephen I. Kings from the House of Árpád ruled until 1301, when the male line of succession died out. Fourteen kings of different houses ruled from 1301 to 1540, including Louis the Great and Matthias Corvinus, both of whom figure in the folktales here.

During the reign of King Louis II (1516–1526), the Ottoman Turks appeared at the southern borders of the country. Indecisive battles were fought until 1526, when Suleiman the Magnificent utterly defeated the Hungarians at the battle of Mohács and plundered the country. In 1541 Suleiman again came to Hungary, encamped below the city of Buda, and strolled into the castle without resistance. With this the capital of Hungary came into Turkish hands, where it remained for almost a century and a half (1541–1686).

Simultaneously, Austria's House of Hapsburg claimed the Hungarian crown and ruled the western part of the country. In 1686, when the Ottoman Empire was forced back to the Balkans, Hungary became part of the Austrian Empire with its western European culture. When the Austro-Hungarian monarchy collapsed following World War I, the Treaty of Trianon (1920) stipulated new borders. Hungary was reduced to a third of its former size and its inhabitants shrank to two-fifths their former number.

Full of turmoil, the twentieth century tested Hungary with German occupation, Soviet Communist domination, a failed revolution in 1956, and more. Through all these the strong spirit of the Hungarian people prevailed, just as it does in these old tales in which brains have triumphed over brawn, and the mighty and mean-spirited have "had it to pay," as the tales say. The lessons these stories teach are about the Hungarian zest for life and the courage to tackle even seven-headed dragons. In this sense they are living tales, and many today have even found their way into cartoon series on Hungarian television.

Following each story are comments which will, I hope, inform the individual tale with historical background, interesting sidelights, or the like. These are meant to tell a little more about Hungary and Hungarians. Finally, the names are presented here last name first as they are in Hungarian.

To write more is to tell all. The tales themselves must do this.

King Matthias and the Old Man

King *Matthias was kind to everyone,* and he liked to talk to those whom he met along the road. Once he and his nobles came upon an old man who had served in his army as a youth. The king recognized him, because he never forgot anyone who had served him.

"Growing old with honesty?" asked the king.

"Thanks to my wife!" replied the old man.

"How much money are you working for?" asked the king.

"For six," replied the old man.

"How much do you spend for living?" asked the king.

"Two," he answered.

"What do you do with the other four?" asked the king.

"I throw them into the mud."

"How many are left from your thirty-two?" asked the king.

"Only twelve."

"Can you milk a billy goat?" asked the king.

1

"Yes, I can."

The noblemen were astounded. They had heard the conversation but had not understood a word.

Observing the situation, the king said to the old man, "Do not explain our conversation to anyone until you see my face again."

At this, the king left with his riding companions. The noblemen inquired at once, "Your Majesty, we heard your conversation with the old man, but we did not understand a thing you were saying. Please explain it to us."

"You have to guess its meaning. Whoever can explain it will be well rewarded," the king answered.

The noblemen thought and thought but could not discover the explanation. Later they went back to the old man to seek it. They urged him and urged him to tell, but all to no avail.

"I cannot say a word until I see the image of the king," said the old man.

"Where? What image?" asked the nobles.

"That image which is imprinted on gold coins," said the old man.

They agreed to pay him ten gold coins and counted them out into his hand.

The old man began the interpretation: "'Growing old in honesty' means that my wife does my laundry. Clean clothes mean honesty. I am honest, that is, I have clean clothes, thanks to my wife."

"But why do you throw four of your six coins earned into the mud? How can you make sense out of that?" they continued.

"Yes, I earn six gold coins a month. With two I live, and I

spend four on my son's education. Because he plays rather than studies, it is like throwing the coins into the mud."

"And what is the meaning of the question, 'How many are left from your thirty-two?'" they asked.

"I will tell you for ten more gold pieces," said the old man.

"Agreed," the nobles said and counted them out into his hand.

The old man laughed and said, "When I was a young man in the king's army, I had thirty-two teeth. Now I have only twelve."

"Here are ten more gold pieces," they said. "Now tell us how anyone can possibly milk a billy goat. Only a nanny goat has milk."

"The explanation is simple," said the old man. "You are the billy goats, and I have milked you out of thirty gold coins. The king's intention was to help me, his former servant, in my old age."

Matthias Hunyadi Corvinus ascended the throne of Hungary in January, 1458, at age fifteen. He was not of royal lineage, but he was the son of Hunyadi János, the most eminent general of fifteenth century Europe, who stamped his individuality on the age more effectively than its crowned kings.

The king's election happened in a picturesque manner. Forty thousand men of the lesser nobility, led by Szilágyi Mihály, encamped below the castle of Buda in the middle of the deeply frozen Danube River and chose

Matthias Hunyadi Corvinus as king. The whole nation joyfully celebrated the event.

Matthias was not an ordinary child, the royal historian, Bonfini, wrote about him. "From his early childhood Matthias was trained to tackle difficulties. He was born on the battlefield in the midst of war cries. As a young boy he learned how to fight through a siege, to cross the Danube River swimming, to spend day and night in full armor in heat and frost, to endure fatigue, hunger, and thirst, to hate cowardice and idleness." As king he did not remain idle, but listened to the advice of his tutor, Vitéz János, who was the most talented politician of that time. During Matthias' reign the civilization in Hungary came close to that of the most civilized European countries. The king had a deep appreciation for the sciences and arts. He used to say, "An uneducated king is a crowned donkey." His library, the Bibliotheca Corviniana, developed into the best collection in Europe and was among the first to be founded.

On April 5, 1490, at the age of forty-seven, Matthias was carried away by death. Posterity mourned him and elevated him into a folk hero. Matthias was "The Just One," who shamed the greedy rich and succored the poor.

King Matthias and the Szekler's Daughter

O*ne day King Matthias* had an idea of how to test the abilities of his people. He called a faithful servant and said, "You know that large stone beside the road? Go stand there and stop all the travelers who pass by and say to them, 'Whoever is able to skin this stone will receive a royal reward.'"

The servant went and stood by the stone and said to all who passed by, "Whoever can skin this stone will receive a royal reward."

Some stopped but did not try skinning the stone. They had never heard that a stone had skin. Others stopped and, tempted by the promise of a royal reward, tried without success.

Later in the day a Szekler and his daughter passed that way. The servant called out to them, "Whoever can skin this stone will receive a royal reward."

The daughter looked the situation over and said to her

father, "Father, please go to Buda to King Matthias and tell him that the stone must first be put to death before we can skin it." Although he did not understand, the Szekler did not want to refuse his daughter. He agreed and set out to see the king.

King Matthias was surprised at the strange request. Not even he had heard of putting a stone to death. He asked, "Where did you get this idea? What a shrewd Szekler you are!"

Not wanting to take the credit, the man told the king that the idea was his daughter's.

The king was pleased with his honest answer and gave the Szekler some gold coins. Then he gave him two nuts and said, "Take these nuts to your daughter and tell her to plant them in a place where no trees grow. After they have grown, tell her to come here to receive a royal reward. Perhaps I will even marry such a bright girl."

The Szekler returned to his daughter, gave her the nuts, and said, "Now the king has given you an even more difficult task."

She just smiled, cracked the nuts, and ate them. "Now," she said, "they are in a place where no trees grow."

In the meantime, the servant had returned to the palace and the skinning of the stone was all but forgotten. However, King Matthias had not forgotten about the girl. Every day he expected her to come to the palace.

At just the right time, the girl said to her father, "Now you can go to the king and tell him that the two nuts have grown. They are here on my chest."

The Szekler went again to Buda and gave the king his daughter's message. The king pondered the message and said,

"Take these two pieces of hemp yarn and tell your daughter to make headbands for everyone in the palace. She is not permitted to use more than these two pieces." And the king gave him some gold coins.

Taking the two pieces of hemp yarn and the small bag of gold coins, the Szekler returned home. He was sure that this test would be too much for his daughter, clever though she was.

At home he repeated the king's instructions and said, "Now you have trouble enough!"

The girl smiled, went out into the backyard and brought in two pieces of wood shavings. Then she said, "Go back to the king and tell him that from these two pieces of wood shavings he has to make a loom, winch, and shuttle for me that I may weave the headbands."

Again the Szekler went to Buda to the king. By now King Matthias was becoming very impressed with the intelligence of the girl. Again he proposed a test. He said, "Tell your daughter that my attic is filled with wineskins which are full of holes. If she can patch them, she will get a prince for a husband."

When her father told her of the latest test, she said, "Tell the king that I will gladly patch the wineskins if he first turns them inside out, because patching doesn't look nice if sewn on the outside."

Again the Szekler went to Buda to the king, who again was amazed at her response. This time he said, "Tell her now to come to Buda, walking neither on the road nor by the wayside, neither dressed nor naked. If she is as hardworking as she is intelligent, I will take her to be my wife."

The king continued, "She has to bring me a gift without bringing me a gift. When she enters the palace gate, she has to greet me as if she didn't."

Back home the Szekler said to his daughter, "This time you are in a great, great trouble."

She smiled, went out into the backyard, caught a sparrow, and put it in a net bag. Then she said, "This will be the gift."

Then she put on her father's fishing net in place of a dress and began the trip with her father's donkey walking in front of her. She held the donkey's tail and carefully fit her steps into its hoof prints. In this way she walked neither on the road nor by the wayside.

Upon entering the palace gate, the girl bowed her head to the king but did not say a word. In this way she greeted him without greeting him. Wearing a fishnet, she was neither dressed nor naked. Then she presented the sparrow in the net bag as a gift, but the top of the bag was open and the sparrow flew away, leaving the king with no gift.

Seeing that she was very beautiful as well as intelligent and industrious, King Matthias embraced the maiden and proposed marriage. They had a truly royal wedding banquet, and as much wine flowed as water in the Danube River below the palace.

King Matthias and the Szekler's daughter lived happily until they had a misunderstanding. It happened in this way: When the annual fair was held in Buda, people came from all over the country in their horse-drawn wagons, which were parked side by side, wheel to wheel. While thus parked, a poor man's mare gave birth under the adjoining wagon. When the mare's owner wanted to take the newborn foal, the owner of the wagon claimed that it belonged to him. Unable to agree, the two men took their dispute to the king, who, lacking evidence other than their word, said that the colt belonged to the man under whose wagon it was.

The loser decided to take his case to the queen, who had quite a reputation for wisdom. She advised him: "Go, get a rowboat and a fishing net. Take them to a field where there is only sand and pretend to be fishing in the sand. When the king passes by, he will see what you are doing and ask why you are fishing where there are no fish. You will tell him, "My lord, you are right. No fish can be found in the sand, and no wagon can give birth to a foal."

He did as she instructed him, and the king said exactly what she knew he would say, and the poor man said exactly what he was told to say. Seeing the rightness of his case, the king changed his decision and granted the man his foal.

Knowing that only the queen could have advised the poor man in this way, the king was very angry with her for his embarrassment. He was so angry, in fact, that he ordered her out of the palace.

She knew that he was quick-tempered and said quietly, "I will leave as soon as possible. Only, I have one request. May I take from the palace what I love most?"

"You have your request," King Matthias replied coldly.

With that she moved out of the palace into a small hut without windows. That night, knowing that the king was sleeping very soundly, she went to his room with four strong men, who lifted the king from his bed by the four corners of his quilt and moved him into the hut.

In the morning when King Matthias awakened, he was confused and did not know where he was. Seeing his wife, he asked, "Where am I? Who did this?"

She said, "You gave me permission to take from the palace what I love most. I love you the most, so during the night I took you to be with me."

The king immediately forgot his anger of the previous day, and afterward they lived in joy and good understanding. They are still living that way, if they haven't died.

The Szeklers are an ethnic group of Hun-Scythian origin, the ancient inhabitants of the eastern part of Transylvania (now Romania). After the disintegration of Attila the Hun's empire (453 A.D.), his sons Csaba and Aladár fought for supremacy. Prince Csaba won the first battle but was defeated in the second. Three thousand soldiers of Csaba's army withdrew with their families to the Carpathians, especially to the wooded area of the snow-covered Harghita Mountains. They called themselves Szeklers to escape the stigma of being Huns.

KING MATTHIAS AND HIS TRUTHFUL SHEPHERD

Once upon a time a Persian king and his daughter visited King Matthias. They were royally welcomed. After a time the purpose of their visit became clear.

The Persian king asked, "Is it true that you have a lamb with golden wool?"

"Yes, it is true," said King Matthias. "Among my flock I have a lamb with golden wool. What is even more remarkable, I have a shepherd who has never told a lie in all his life."

"Then he has never been properly tested," said the Persian king. "I will show you that I can get him to lie."

"You can test him, but I am sure that he will not lie," replied King Matthias.

"I am sure that I can deceive him and get him to lie," insisted the guest.

"I bet you up to half of my kingdom that he will not lie," said King Matthias.

"Agreed. I bet you up to half of my kingdom that he will."

They shook hands and the Persian king retired to his suite. There he took off his royal robe and put on peasant clothes. Then he went out into the field and greeted the shepherd.

"Welcome, my lord the king," responded the shepherd.

"How did you know that I am a king?" asked the king.

"I recognized you by your speech. Only a king speaks as you speak," replied the shepherd.

"I will give you a heap of gold coins, six horses, and a carriage if you will give me the lamb with golden wool," said the Persian king.

"Sir, I would not give it for the whole world. King Matthias would hang me if I were to give it to you," said the shepherd.

At this the king offered him even more, but the faithful shepherd still would not accept. Failing in his attempt, the king retired to his chambers, where his daughter noticed his sadness.

"Oh, Father, do not be so sad," said the princess. "I myself will go. You will see that I will succeed."

She took a box of gold coins and a bottle of wine sweetened with honey. With these, she thought, she would surely succeed.

When the princess offered to buy the lamb, the shepherd said that he had all the money he needed and that King Matthias would hang him if he were to give her the lamb with the golden wool.

Little by little she let him drink from her wine sweetened with honey. After a time the shepherd was in high spirits and promised to give her the lamb if she would promise to marry him. He knew that a princess must keep her word.

Hesitatingly, the princess promised.

"Kill the lamb, skin it, eat the meat yourself, and give me the fleece," she instructed.

The shepherd followed her instructions, and the princess was happy to take the lambskin to her father, who was overwhelmed with her cunning.

The next morning the shepherd was very sorry for what he had done. What would he tell King Matthias about the loss of the lamb with the golden wool? He set out to the palace to give an account, but along the way he stopped, stuck his shepherd's crook into a mole hill, and put his hat on top of it. Then he envisioned his conversation with his king:

"What brings you to the palace, and what is the news from the fields?" the king would ask.

"I have bad news, sir. The lamb with the golden wool has been devoured by a wolf," he would reply.

The very thought of telling the king a lie frightened him. The king would detect it immediately and say, "You have never lied to me before. Why are you lying to me now? If a wolf devoured one sheep, he would have devoured others also."

Putting on his hat and taking his crook in his hand, the shepherd continued toward the palace, all the while making up imaginary conversations with his king:

"What brings you to the palace, and what is the news from the fields?"

"I have bad news, sir. The lamb with the golden wool has fallen into a deep pit and died."

Again he heard the king say, "You have never lied to me before. Why are you lying to me now? If it fell into a deep pit, why haven't others fallen into it before?"

A third time he foresaw an imaginary conversation:

"What brings you to the palace, and what is the news from the fields?"

"I have bad news, sir. The lamb with the golden wool has been stolen."

"You have never lied to me before. Why are you lying now? If it was stolen, why weren't others stolen also?"

Worried and troubled about the whole affair, the shepherd arrived at the palace. Although it was dinnertime, he was determined not to delay the matter. He entered and found his king, the Persian king, and his daughter sitting at the table. He began by paying homage to them. He did not know that the Persian king had given the lambskin with the golden wool to King Matthias.

As was his custom, King Matthias asked, "What brings you to the palace, and what is the news from the fields?"

They were all waiting to see if the shepherd would lie. One king or the other was about to lose half his kingdom.

"Little else, sir, except that I exchanged the lambskin with the golden wool for a beautiful Persian lamb," he replied.

King Matthias was overjoyed and ordered, "Bring that lamb in."

"My lord, she is already here. She is sitting between you and the Persian king. She agreed to become my wife in exchange for the lambskin with the golden wool."

"Long live my truthful shepherd!" exclaimed King

Matthias. "You did not lie even though you knew that it could have cost you your life. For this I will give you the half of the kingdom which I have just won from the Persian king."

"And I will give my daughter to you in marriage!" exclaimed the Persian king. "There is not another like you in this whole world."

Marry they did, and half the Persian kingdom became theirs to rule. Perhaps they are still ruling there, if they have not died in the meantime.

A whole volume of King Matthias legends is available in Hungarian, and some of the stories exist in forty-five versions. Matthias was as wise as the biblical King Solomon and equally at home among kings and peasants. During his rule Hungary flourished; only later did part of it fall to Turkish rule.

One-Time Dog Market at Buda

A*lthough it happened* more than five hundred years ago, many people still remember the dog market at Buda. Whenever they think of it, they laugh, and for good reason.

During the reign of Matthias the Just, a wealthy man lived in a village near Buda. He made sport of people and loved to mock them. Ridiculing others was his main source of pleasure—after his money, of course.

Once this wealthy man made a good business deal at Buda at a market just west of the Danube River. He returned home with a pouch full of gold coins and bragged to everyone that he had made the money by selling dogs.

A poor man heard about this and went to him, asking for the details of his success. To make a fool of the poor man, the rich man said, "Not long ago I had some business at Buda. While there I learned that the king is paying a good price for dogs. It seems that he needs a lot of them. I immediately bought a pack of good dogs and took them to the king. See, here is the pouch of gold that he paid for them. If you had a head for business, you, too, could take advantage of this opportunity and escape your poverty."

The poor man believed the lie and could not rest for the thought of a pouch of gold. Selling his only possession, a cow, he bought as many good dogs as he could.

Things went well until he arrived at the castle gate in Buda. When the guards drove him and his dogs away, the poor man cursed the wealthy man for his lie.

Fortunately, King Matthias was looking out his window at the time and observed the poor man's plight. He ordered a servant to invite the fellow in for an audience.

Taken before the king, the poor man explained how he had been deceived and how he had sold his only cow with the hope of escaping his poverty. The king understood and had compassion on him, giving him a hundred gold pieces. Also, he had the name of the deceiver recorded for future punishment.

How happily the poor man went home! He, too, bragged about the good dog market at Buda.

When the rich man heard that his neighbor had indeed taken dogs to the king and had come home with a hundred gold pieces, his envy and greed took control of him. He bought as many good dogs as he could find and headed for the castle.

Like the poor man, the guards stopped him at the gate. Fearing financial ruin, he let out an ear-piercing scream.

Hearing his bellowing, King Matthias looked out the window, saw the dogs, and understood what was going on. He

ordered his servant to invite the man for an audience, knowing that the greedy fellow had fallen into his own pit.

"My good sir," the king addressed him. "I am sorry that you let such a fine opportunity slip through your fingers. You are simply too late. The dog market at Buda happened only once."

Buda is the old city on the west bank of the Danube River, which separated it from the city of Pest on the east bank. Bridges made possible the uniting of the two cities into Budapest in 1896. To this day, the king's remark is proverbial in Hungary. When people say, "The dog market happened only once at Buda," they mean that something was a unique opportunity.

King Matthias and the Weatherman

One day *King Matthias* invited his weatherman to go for a walk with him. As they set out, King Matthias asked, "Are we going to get some rain?"

"No, no, we won't, sir. The conditions just aren't right. It will be a fair day," replied the weatherman.

A shepherd walking behind them heard the conversation and said, "My lord, I think that it will rain. My donkey brayed, and that always means rain."

Dismissing the shepherd's prognosis, King Matthias and his weatherman continued on their walk. Soon a black cloud appeared and a heavy shower soaked them to the skin.

After the rain stopped, King Matthias turned to his weatherman and said, "The truth is that the donkey is a good weatherman and the weatherman is a big donkey."

Humor stories about King Matthias are very much loved. Szép Ernő collected and published forty-two such humor stories; ours is one of them.

Together with fantasy, humor helped the Hungarian peasantry to cope with the harshness of life. Although the feudal period has long passed, the Hungarian sense of humor has remained. Even during the Communist era, Hungary had its humor theaters, clubs, and magazines. Today, when friends meet, their conversation often begins with the question, "Have you heard this joke?"

THE QUICK-WITTED COBBLER AT WITS' END

"**W**oe is me!* My head is throbbing and I'm cold," lamented Rózsi, the wife of Mr. Varga, the cobbler.

"You must be sick. You're shivering so badly that the bed is shaking. I'll cover you with my fur coat," said Mr. Varga.

He gave her a mug of mulled wine and tried all the other home remedies he'd ever heard of. Instead of getting better, she got worse. Now they started wailing in chorus.

"If nothing helps, I have to find a city doctor," he thought.

Without further delay Mr. Varga put bread and bacon into his satchel and set out to the big city. It was almost dark when he got there, so he spent the night at an inn. Early in the morning the innkeeper gave him directions to find a doctor. He walked and walked until he found a big house with a fancy shingle on the wall. He went closer and examined the copper shingle. He couldn't understand a word because it was written in Latin. It had to be the doctor's house.

Mr. Varga entered and found himself in a large waiting room full of people. This meant a long wait. When he was called, he was still wearing his fur cap. People were amazed at his lack of manners. The doctor's helper told him to remove his cap, and he apologetically did. Upon entering the doctor's office, he looked around and carefully observed everything.

The doctor asked, "What is wrong with you?"

The cobbler responded, "My wife is very sick. She has a very bad headache and shivers."

"And where is she now? Why isn't she here?" asked the doctor.

"She couldn't come because she is too sick, so I came instead to ask you for a prescription."

"I'm not permitted to write a prescription without seeing the patient," explained the doctor and shooed him out the door.

Mr. Varga was sad. Retrieving his fur cap, he saw another patient leave the doctor's office with a prescription in his hand. This gave him an idea.

Catching up with the man, Mr. Varga asked, "What did you pay for this prescription?"

"Five forints."

"What's it for?"

"I have chills, fever, and a headache."

"I will offer you a bargain. Why don't you sell me that prescription for ten forints? You can get another for only five."

"No, no," said the man with the prescription.

"Then at least let me see what is written on it," begged the cobbler. "My wife has the same symptoms, but the doctor wouldn't give me a prescription without seeing her."

It seemed like scribbling, but he copied it carefully. Mr. Varga was pleased to have a prescription that cost him nothing. He went happily to the apothecary and handed his scribbling to him.

The young apothecary was not embarrassed that he could not read the poor handwriting. He always had a bottle of freshly brewed camomile tea handy to fill unreadable prescriptions. He charged only two forints for the bottle of tea with its unreadable label.

As soon as Mr. Varga arrived home, he gave a spoonful of that liquid to his wife and before bedtime, another. Next morning she was ready to get up and prepare breakfast. He was glad to see her up and around, and he was convinced that the medicine had made her well.

"I know what I'm going to do," said the cobbler. "This county has no doctor but too many cobblers. No one will notice if there is one less cobbler. But a doctor can make a great difference. I will be that doctor," he announced proudly.

Rózsi felt well enough to start arguing. "Can you imagine what great learning a doctor must have, and you can hardly read and write! A cobbler should stick to his last," she said sternly.

"Being a doctor is also a trade. I saw it yesterday. All I need is to hang out a copper shingle on a big house and furnish the office like this: put a desk in the middle, cover it with small pieces of paper for prescriptions, have bookshelves with lots of books and wear doctor's clothes. And I need a woman to call the patients and to remind them to take off their hats before going in to see the doctor. I noticed everything while I was waiting." Mr. Varga was confident.

"Where can you get money to do all that?" Rózsi asked eagerly.

"I have a plan. I will make a pair of boots for King Louis the Great. A royal reward can pay the expenses to open my doctor's office."

He selected his best piece of leather, measured it, drew the design, and cut out the pieces. He sewed, nailed, and glued until the boots took shape. When he put the finishing stitches on them, the winter was over and the snow had melted. The weather was mild enough for the long walk to the capital city. The cobbler packed some food, put the exquisite boots into his bag, and left. He promised his wife that he would return a rich man.

It took many days to arrive at the royal palace. The palace gates were closely guarded, and there was no royal road for a poor cobbler to enter. Only those with a good reason were permitted to do so.

Mr. Varga explained that his coming was important because he brought a gift for the king with the hope of receiving a royal reward.

At this the gatekeeper softened, "If you share the reward with me, I will let you in."

Mr. Varga had no other choice, so he agreed. When he got to the door of the throne room, he was asked again about his purpose. He knew already that he had to promise the other half of his reward to this doorkeeper. He did.

Finally Mr. Varga was admitted into the presence of King Louis. He came forward, paid his homage to His Majesty, and offered the gift.

The king looked at the boots, tried them on, and they fit him perfectly. He had a royal time walking on the red carpet in his new boots. He ordered the treasurer to pay a hundred pieces of gold to such a skilled craftsman.

Mr. Varga thanked the king for his generosity but asked if he could receive a hundred lashes instead, assuring the king that he would soon understand such an unusual request.

"If you are serious, you may have your request," said the king.

A soldier brought the whipping bench and whip and was ready to do his job.

Mr. Varga called the doorman. "Do you still insist on receiving half of the royal reward?" he asked.

When the unwary doorman replied yes, the soldier strapped him to the bench and gave him fifty lashes in the presence of the king.

"Now call the gatekeeper," requested Mr. Varga.

"Do you still insist on receiving half of the royal reward?" he asked.

When the unwary gatekeeper replied yes, he received his fifty lashes.

King Louis was pleased with the punishment of his corrupt servants and ordered the treasurer to reward the quick-witted cobbler with two hundred pieces of gold.

As soon as Mr. Varga arrived home with the royal gold, he proceeded to arrange for his doctor's practice. First he paid a visit to the coppersmith and ordered an expensive copper shingle with the words: "Dr. Varga will shape up anybody whose body is out of shape."

The coppersmith was amazed at such a claim and asked, "Can you shape up a quarrelsome mother-in-law?"

"All she needs is a change of air. Send her over the Carpathian Mountains, where nobody will understand her language. That will cure her of the quarreling habit," advised the now-Dr. Varga.

A few days of visiting in the neighborhood where he had purchased a big house made him confident of his coming success. Before opening day, he admired his appearance in the clean window-glass and noticed that he needed a haircut.

"Only three blocks from here I saw a barbershop," he thought. He walked there as fast as he could, because it was lunchtime already. A young apprentice barber welcomed him.

"Where is your master?" asked Dr. Varga.

"He's upstairs in his dental office. During his lunch break he pulls teeth," said the talkative young man.

Dr. Varga was not surprised by this remark. He smiled understandingly. "That's right," he thought. "The cobbler becomes a medical doctor, and the barber makes a good dentist."

On a quiet Monday morning, Dr. Varga was ready to open his office. The copper shingle was enough for advertising, and the coppersmith had spread the news about the miraculous healing of his quarrelsome mother-in-law.

Dr. Varga's simple treatments healed many who were suffering from obscure ailments. That made him happy and content.

He thought to himself, "Those who get well are thankful, and those with difficult cases I send to the real doctors in the city."

By the time Dr. Varga had reached the apex of his quackery, the bubonic plague struck the country. It first broke out in Transylvania, killing one third of the population. Even the king became gravely ill, but recovered. The queen fell victim to the plague; no doctor could help her. Even doctors of great learning were not able to stop the plague. Dr. Varga's office was filled with desperately sick people, but he could not help them.

In this awful distress he said, "I am at my wits' end. I don't know what to do. People are dying, and I can't help them. I just am not a real doctor."

"But you do know what to do," said Rózsi. "The king has recovered from his illness, and he may need a new pair of boots. It is as I told you when you first thought of becoming a doctor: 'The cobbler should stick to his last.'"

"You are right, my dear," said the now-Mr. Varga. "My name means cobbler, and that is what I am. I will stick to my last until my last breath."

This story pokes a lot of fun at doctors and it has passed through many tellers, right up into the twentieth century, when it appears to have been modernized. But it is also set in a Golden Age, and rightly called so.

The forty-year reign of Louis the Great (1342–1382), who extended his empire, was a beautiful period when three seas washed the borders of Hungary—the Baltic, the Black Sea, and the Adriatic. The only dark spot on this age was the bubonic plague. The Black Death was one of the greatest pestilences in recorded history, ultimately killing as much as three-quarters of the people in Europe and Asia. It struck the Mediterranean countries first. From Italy the plague was carried across the Alps and raged throughout Europe until 1400. Hungary was not immune.

THE SHEPHERD OF RABBITS

Long ago in a place not seen by anyone now living dwelled a king who had a beautiful daughter. When she became of marriageable age, the king made a proclamation calling all the rich and eligible young nobles to come to seek her hand. And come they did from all quarters of Europe and other continents: tall and short, thin and fat, stupid and intelligent, cultured and uncouth.

The princess gave each one the same test. She threw a golden apple as hard and as high into the air as she could. Just as a suitor saw it on its way down, it seemed to disappear in thin air. Not one who came succeeded in catching it.

At the end of the last day, the princess threw the apple as before. Seemingly out of nowhere, a tall and handsome young man unknown to anyone reached up his hand. No one saw the apple descend, but lo! it was in his hand as if directed there by magic powers.

The king was very displeased, because the young man was not of noble blood. He said to him, "You have passed only the first test. There is yet another, and it will not be so easy."

"Your Majesty, for the princess I would pass two more tests, if necessary," he replied.

"This is the test," said the king. "If you can guard my rabbits, you will have gained your prize. If not, you will have it to pay."

The young man was sorry. He knew nothing about rabbits and had never guarded any before. While the king was at breakfast, he sat in the portico thinking about his desperate situation.

While the young stranger was pondering his fate, the Rabbit Spirit in the form of an old woman appeared before him. She said, "Don't worry about the test. Here is a silver whistle. Whenever you need to call or rescue a rabbit, just blow it and the rabbit will return to you immediately."

He thanked her for it, and even while he was looking at her, she disappeared before his very eyes. "Strange," he thought, "but providential."

The unwanted time arrived. The rabbits had never been free from their hutches; so when they were released in the pasture, they raced to the four winds.

Remembering the words of the old woman, the young man blew the silver whistle. As if by magic every one of them turned on its hind legs and lined up around him like a soldier at attention. Come what may, they would not leave him.

The king was watching from an upper palace window.

When he saw what had happened, he wondered who this young man was that even the rabbits obeyed him.

Not wanting the young man to succeed, at least not so easily, the king said to his daughter, "Go and dress like a poor peasant woman. Then take a bag with you, walk out into the pasture and ask the rabbit shepherd for a rabbit. In this way he will have one rabbit too few when he brings them in for the night."

Not knowing the situation, the princess readily agreed.

The young man saw her coming in the distance. From her walk he knew that she was no ordinary woman. In fact, he could tell that she was of noble blood. Yet why, he wondered, was she dressed like a peasant?

As she approached, she greeted him, "Good afternoon, rabbit shepherd. I have never seen a rabbit shepherd before."

"Good afternoon, noble lady," he replied. "What brings you here?"

"Why do you greet me so?" she asked. "You can see that I am only a poor peasant. I beg you to give me one of your rabbits."

"I will give you one, noble lady, but in return you must give me a kiss," he said.

"Sir, you are quite mistaken. I am not a princess. Why do you want to kiss a poor woman?"

The young man knew, however, which way the wind was blowing and said again, "A kiss for a rabbit. That is the bargain."

The princess wanted very much to please her father with a rabbit, so she reluctantly kissed the shepherd. She was sur-

prised at how tender his kiss was and felt strangely attracted to him. She opened the bag, and he put in a rabbit. "Ah," she thought. "Success."

The princess was only halfway to the palace when the shepherd blew the silver whistle. Unbeknownst to her, the rabbit jumped out of the bag and returned to the shepherd.

As soon as the princess entered the palace, the king said, "I saw from the window that you got a rabbit. Please show it to me."

She proudly opened the bag, but they found no rabbit.

"Oh, Father, I begged for a rabbit, and I thought that he put one into the bag. Now I see that he deceived me." She did not want to disclose that she had kissed the shepherd in exchange for a rabbit.

"Come, come. Think nothing of it. You are young. I will test him myself. You will see that I will succeed," the king boasted. He disguised himself as a poor man, mounted a donkey, and rode out into the field.

The young man saw him coming in the distance. From the gait of the donkey he could tell that it was no ordinary donkey. Only royalty had trained donkeys.

"How are you doing, young shepherd?" asked the king.

"Good afternoon, noble sir," replied the shepherd. "I am just tending the king's rabbits as he instructed me to do."

"Why do you greet me so, young shepherd? You can see that I am only a poor man," said the king. "Please have pity on a hungry old man and give me one of your many rabbits."

"Noble sir," replied the young man, "I will give you one rabbit if you will kiss the place under the donkey's tail."

Driven by his desire to deceive the young man, the king reluctantly raised the donkey's tail and kissed the dreaded spot. Thereupon, the young man dropped one of the rabbits into the waiting bag.

Overjoyed, the king jumped into the saddle and rode off as fast as he could in the direction of the palace. When he was halfway there, the shepherd blew the silver whistle, and the rabbit jumped out of the bag and returned to him.

The princess was waiting for her father, who could hardly wait to show her his rabbit. Yet, when he opened the bag, there was none.

"Oh, dear daughter, I begged for a rabbit, and I thought that he put one into the bag. Now I see that he deceived even me," said the king. He did not want to disclose that he had kissed the dreaded place under the donkey's tail in exchange for a rabbit.

That evening the shepherd of rabbits came to the royal barn where the rabbit hutches were. All one hundred rabbits were lined up behind him like so many soldiers. Then he reported to the king.

"I see that you are an unusual young man," said the king. "You outwitted both the princess and me today. You agreed to pass yet another test, if necessary. If you succeed this time, I cannot deny giving the princess to you as your wife. If you fail, however, you will have it to pay. The test is this: You have to tell enough lies to fill this sack."

Thinking that he had met his end, the young man racked his brain. Even if he could think of enough lies, how could he put them in a sack?

The king called his advisers, and they formed a circle around the young man, who sat there with the open sack in front of him.

Then he began. He told every lie that he had ever heard of. Surely they were enough!

When he looked at the king questioningly, the king said, "Continue. The sack is not even half full."

"Continue I will, noble sir," said the young man. And he began again.

"When I was the shepherd of rabbits, the princess came to me disguised as a poor peasant woman and begged for a rabbit. I told her that I would give her a rabbit in exchange for a kiss. When she kissed me, I kissed her ever so tenderly."

At this the princess turned scarlet red.

"After that," he continued, "the king came to me disguised as a poor man and begged for a rabbit. I told him that I would give him a rabbit if he would kiss that dreaded place beneath his donkey's tail. He kissed it, and I gave him the rabbit."

Now the king turned scarlet red.

"Enough! Enough! Enough of these lies," the king shouted, looking nervously around him. "The sack is more than full."

The king called the princess and the young man into the privacy of his quarters. "Young man, you have more than shown yourself worthy of marrying the princess. As soon as we can make the preparations for a wedding befitting a princess and the heir to the throne, you shall be wed."

For her part, the princess had never been happier.

As stories go, the king gave a royal wedding and banquet

for them. Rich and poor alike from near and far came and celebrated at the king's expense for a whole week.

Also, as stories go, the young couple lived many years in peace and happiness. Perhaps they are still living so, if they have not died in the meantime.

The story was first collected and published by the famous folklorist and writer Benedek Elek (1859–1929) under the title, "The King's Rabbits." Benedek's folktale collections ran into several editions during the last century. He was a passionate educator. Every children's textbook contained something written by him. Among Hungarian children he was and still is known as "Grandpa" Benedek.

This story has many similarities to "King Matthias and His Truthful Shepherd." The theme of scheming aristocrats being made fun of by nimble-minded peasants is a favorite one in many European folktales. Humor was one way for poor people to triumph in a tightly structured society.

Peter's Taller Tale

Farther away than can be imagined lived a man with three very handsome sons. On a certain day the king of that place issued a proclamation stating that he would give his daughter in marriage to the young man who could tell the most unbelievable tall tale.

The oldest son, Peter, was so handsome that looking at him was like looking at the sun. Hearing of the king's proclamation, he set out for the royal palace. More princes than stars in the sky and more noblemen than sand on the seashore wanted to marry the princess, who was so beautiful that she could turn herself into all the colors of the rainbow. Yet not one of them had been able to tell a really unbelievable tall tale to the king's satisfaction.

Now it was Peter's turn. He hoped it would be worth the long journey and the even longer wait. Upon entering the royal chamber, he paid his respects to His Majesty.

"What brings a humble lad here to the court?" asked the king.

"Your Majesty," said Peter, "you have offered the princess in marriage to the young man who can tell the most unbelievable tall tale. I would like to try, sir. Nothing ventured, nothing gained."

"Can you provide for a wife?" said the king kindly, thinking all the while that the young man could not.

"Only God knows, sir. I would try to support her somehow. My father has a house and farmland," Peter replied.

"I believe it," said the king.

"We have two oxen and a cow," Peter continued.

"I believe this, also," said the king.

"Recently we had an accumulation of manure so great that it overflowed into our backyard," Peter went on.

"I believe it."

"My two brothers and I transported the manure to the fields on two wagons and it took two weeks," said Peter.

"I believe it."

"When our father went to inspect the job we had done, he discovered that we had put the manure on our neighbor's land by mistake," continued Peter.

"I believe it."

"'What shall we do now?' our father asked. 'Do any of you have any ideas?'"

"I had an idea, Your Majesty. This is what we did. The four of us went one to each of the four corners of our neighbor's land and moved it like a tablecloth over our land. Then we sowed seed on it. Soon a dense oak forest grew on that place.

No one had ever seen such a beautiful forest before. That fall the acorns were so abundant that we had to buy a herd of pigs to eat them."

"I believe all that you have said," said the king. "Have you more to say?"

"Yes, Your Majesty. At this point we hired the king's old father to be our swineherd," Peter smiled.

"You are lying, you rascal!" shouted the king angrily.

But then the king realized that Peter had told the most unbelievable tall tale. In keeping with his proclamation, he declared Peter the winning suitor of the princess.

Then began all the preparations for a royal wedding. Guests from seven countries attended the extended festivities. Wine flowed in streams and food was yet more abundant. Even the orphan children in the kingdom ate royally and each one received a piece of wedding cake with his meal.

This tale is based on "The Vain King," retold by Illyés Gyula.

Hungarian nobles, especially kings, were proud of their ancestors. The king had the right to raise anybody to noble rank for reasons sufficient to himself, but the king himself usually was of royal lineage.

Storytellers generally admitted that their tales were not true by using such closing formulas as, "If you don't believe it, go find out for yourself."

GRASSHOPPER

A*lmost no one* knew his real name. From infancy his father had called him "Grasshopper," because instead of crawling like other babies, he leapt like his namesake.

Time passed, and Grasshopper's father enrolled him in school. How he disliked the discipline! His friends were already apprentices or were working in the fields with their fathers. But not him! He groaned at the thought of school but he usually went.

One day Grasshopper left home with his school books under his arm. Instead of going to school, he went to the marketplace, where he found a little nook and sat down to read aloud from a Latin grammar book. He was sure to attract a crowd.

And one gathered. But no one understood a word. Finally, one man summoned the courage to ask, "Who are you? What are you reading? What is the meaning of all this?"

Grasshopper replied, "This book contains ancient wisdom to solve difficult riddles and conundrums."

Just then the king was passing by with his entourage. He had a difficult problem that needed solving, and he overheard the boy. "Perhaps," he thought, "I have found someone to help me."

The king invited Grasshopper to the palace, where he explained the problem. A diamond ring was missing, and he suspected that someone on the palace staff had stolen it.

"My son," he said, "if you find the ring for me, I will give you a thousand gold pieces. It belonged to my grandmother and is to become the possession of the princess when she marries."

Word went throughout the palace that a boy with unusual powers had come to find the thief. Some greeted him as if he were royalty. A shiver went up the spines of others as they contemplated the fate of the thief. But the princess had seen too many charlatans to be impressed.

Counting on his usual luck, Grasshopper toured the palace, greeting everyone politely but viewing them all with suspicion. The scene was set. Everyone was a potential suspect. No one knew what powers he had, and no one knew when he would reveal the thief.

At dinnertime Grasshopper was seated at a table usually used only by the king and queen. The head chef himself came to ask what he wanted to eat and drink.

"First, I want to see your staff," Grasshopper said.

There were three chef's helpers, all dressed in white and all very respectful as they presented themselves one by one.

Knowing that he had to begin with someone, Grasshopper said to the first who entered, "I got you, you rogue."

Then to the second and third he said the same. Little did he know that he had unwittingly found the culprits.

But Grasshopper was not one to let food get cold. While he was relishing pheasant soup, venison roast, dáláuzi for dessert and drinking the king's best Tokay wine, the chef's helpers approached.

"Please do not betray us to the king," they pleaded. "When we heard that you had come, we knew that we would be discovered. For your silence we will each give you a hundred gold coins, and we will give you the ring."

"Very well," Grasshopper said, thrilled that he had found the ring so easily. "The ring is all I want. Bring it to me, and the king won't know a thing about it."

"Now," thought Grasshopper, "what do I tell the king? He will want to know where I found the ring."

He pondered and pondered, and finally an idea came to him. He had seen a goose tied by one leg in the kitchen. It was to be dinner for the royal family. Grasshopper brought the goose to his room, tied it to the bed leg, and put the ring down its gullet. Then he rushed to the king to announce that he had solved the mystery.

"So quickly?" asked the king. "Your powers are amazing! At first I thought you might be only a deceiver. Where, then, is the ring?"

"Come, royal sir, and I will show you," said Grasshopper, bowing low.

Leading the king to the goose, Grasshopper announced with great solemnity, "My mystical powers have shown me that the ring is in the goose's craw."

"Impossible!" exclaimed the king. "Are you absolutely sure?"

"Yes, royal sir, I am. Grasshopper, the solver of mysteries, has never been wrong."

The king ordered the goose to be butchered at once and the craw searched for the ring. Upon seeing it, the king leapt for joy and embraced Grasshopper. "Remarkable, remarkable!" he exclaimed. "Very remarkable!" He immediately ordered the royal treasurer to bring the promised reward.

Even with Grasshopper's success, the princess was not so easily convinced. She asked the triumphant young man to take a walk with her in order to put him to a test. As they strolled through the gardens, she caught a grasshopper while he was not watching.

Then she said to him, "If you really do have such remarkable powers and can find things that others cannot, tell me what I have in my hand."

Grasshopper was caught. He had no idea what the princess held in her hand. Half aloud, he murmured, "Now, Grasshopper, show your wit."

"You are right!" exclaimed the princess. "See! Here is the grasshopper I caught in my hand. Never again will I doubt your powers. As a reward, I will send you to school and I will pay for your scholarship. The only condition is that you report your progress to me."

Trapped by his own scheme, Grasshopper was truly caught. He had no choice but to go to school and become not a grasshopper, but a bookworm.

Until the sixteenth century, education in Hungary was conducted in Latin. Students had to memorize long narratives and the rules of the Latin grammar. The rigors of this system discouraged many students, so it is no wonder that Grasshopper disliked the idea of continuing his education.

This version of the story is based on the tale published in the collection *Hétszázhetvenhét Magyar Népmese.*

KINDNESS REWARDED

B*eyond the seven seas* lived a widow with two young daughters, Boriska and Terka. She worried about Terka, because she used her time for useless things and would not listen to instructions. Boriska, the younger, was different. From early childhood she had worked happily in the house, in the barnyard with the animals, and in the garden. Her energy seemed boundless.

When she grew into young adulthood, she told her mother that she was going to look for a job. In this way she hoped to help the family make a decent living. At first her mother resisted, but she eventually relented and gave Boriska her blessing to go out into the world.

Finding a job in the country was not easy. She walked and walked and walked on the dusty country roads. Once she heard a dog whining and followed the sound to its source. To her surprise, the dog spoke and asked her to pull a thorn from its paw.

She pulled it out, tore a piece of cloth from her scarf, and bandaged the wound.

"Thank you, kind girl," said the dog. "Someday I will repay your kindness."

Boriska continued on. Beside the road she noticed a vineyard unattended. The vines were drooping, and weeds were choking them. Again to her surprise, the vines spoke: "Please, kind girl, put us up on our trellises as we should be and rid us of these weeds. Then we will be able to produce a good crop."

Forgetting her goal of finding a paying job, Boriska busily put the vines up on their trellises and pulled all the weeds. Then, realizing how much time had passed, she hurried on her way.

At a short distance she noticed a well. The work in the hot sun had made her very thirsty, and she wanted a refreshing drink. To her surprise, the well was neglected and full of trash.

Then the well spoke: "Kind girl, my water is very sweet and good, but no one wants it, because so much trash has fallen into me. Please help me by cleaning it out."

Boriska cleaned out the trash, took a deep, refreshing drink, and went on her way. Next she saw an old man who was unable to keep his oven in good repair.

"Kind girl, can you please spare the time to help me?" asked the old man. "You see the condition of my oven, and I can no longer bake my bread in it."

Having helped her mother many times to keep their oven in good condition, she knew exactly what to do. In less than an hour the oven was working as if it were new.

"Thank you, kind girl," said the old man. "May God repay your kindness."

By now it was almost dark. Following the light of a candle in a distant window, Boriska arrived at a small cottage, where she was welcomed by an older couple. She greeted them politely: "Good evening, my kind hosts."

"The same to you, kind girl," they replied. "How did you ever get to such a remote place?"

"I'm looking for a job," she replied, "and my travels have brought me to your door."

"Well, you arrived at just the right place at just the right time. We have been looking in vain for a hardworking servant girl. We see by your hands that you are just such a girl," they said. "In our service there are three days in a year. You will learn later what we mean by this."

"But what are my duties in such a small cottage?" Boriska asked. "Surely there cannot be a lot to do."

"These will be your duties. Prepare a good meal for us every day; early in the morning clean these two rooms thoroughly, and do not enter or even look into the third room, which is our bedroom," they said. "We will pay you well."

"Then you have a servant girl," she said. "I will do all that you say and even more."

The new servant girl got up early each morning, cleaned the two rooms, and prepared whatever her hosts wanted for their meal. She was not even curious about the third room. She always found something to keep her busy.

The first day before the old couple left the house, the

woman gave her these instructions: "For dinner you have to prepare a roast for us. It must be well cooked, but you are not allowed to bake it in our oven or in front of our oven or on our hearth or over open flames."

When they were gone, Boriska began to cry. She had never before heard such instructions. She was desperate and even thought of leaving to find work elsewhere.

While she was debating what to do, the oven spoke: "Listen, kind girl, you don't need to be sad. I know who you are. On your way here you helped an old man by repairing his oven, which was made by the same craftsman who made me. Put the meat on top of me so that it will not be either in me or in front of me. Neither will it be over open flames. In this way the meat will cook slowly and become very tender."

Boriska did as she was told and all the oven had said was true. When the old couple came home that evening, they were amazed that their servant had followed their instructions and yet was able to present them with such an excellent roast.

The second day the old couple was up early, but Boriska was up even earlier and was doing her cleaning. They left her no specific instructions about dinner, but when they returned home in the evening, she served them a delicious meal.

The third day went as the second day. After dinner the woman said, "I am very pleased with you. Never before have we had such a good servant girl. Now we will pay your wages and give you a gift."

She held out two small jewelry boxes. One was very fancy and the other very plain. "You may choose which one you wish," she said.

"I am young and inexperienced," said Boriska. "I will let you choose for me."

"You are young, but you are wise," said the woman. "A foolish girl would have immediately chosen the fancy one, and in this case it would have been a mistake."

In the morning, the old couple said, "You have worked your year for us. Now take your wages and your jewelry box and go home to your mother. She is surely worried about you."

Boriska set out on the road home. On the way, the old man called to her and gave her fresh bread from the oven which she had repaired. A little farther on she came to the well that she had cleaned. As she stooped to get a drink, she saw her face reflected in the water. She had become very beautiful, more beautiful than a rainbow.

As she passed the vineyard, she was surprised to see that the vines were loaded with large, ripe grapes. They called to her and asked her to take as many of their clusters as she wanted for her journey and family.

Hardly able to carry the jewelry box, the bread, and the grapes, Boriska quickened her step so as to arrive home before dark. Just as she came to the place where she had pulled the thorn from the dog's paw, the dog appeared again. He had a fully baked rabbit for her.

Boriska's mother and sister were amazed when she arrived home with fresh baked bread, grapes, a baked rabbit, her wages, and the jewelry box. Their amazement was even greater when they opened the box. As they took out each jewel, another appeared. There was gold and silver, too, and even silk dresses for them all.

They all went to bed happy and slept well. Early next morning when the mother awakened, she heard Boriska singing happily as she worked in the kitchen.

Benedek Elek was one of Hungary's premier folklorists. This tale is based on one which he collected and published under the title, "What Is in the Little Chest?" Benedek dedicated his life to education, becoming the editor of many teachers' and children's publications. Believing that folktales have important educational value, Benedek collected them tirelessly.

This story teaches such moral values as hard work, modesty, resourcefulness, and especially, kindness. The values of the culture were often transmitted by way of such folktales.

HOW A STUDENT
BECAME A KING

In *another time* and place a student set out on the journey to the university. On the way he found some dried peas in a field, picked them up, and put them in one of his pockets. His father had advised him to pick up anything worth more than a flea.

By nightfall he arrived in the capital city, where he presented himself at the royal palace and requested lodging for the night and provisions with which to continue his journey. It was a custom in those days for the king to offer hospitality to travelers, especially to students, because the queen was always on the lookout for a suitable husband for their daughter.

The student was a handsome young man with eloquent speech and impeccable manners. The queen thought that such a young man could not be a simple student traveling to the university. Indeed, she thought, he must really be a prince who wants to remain incognito. Yes, he might even be a suitable match for the princess. So her reasoning went.

The queen told this to the king, who agreed that she could well be right. Wanting to be sure, they decided to put the young man to a test that would surely give them their answer. This would take time, so they invited him to be their guest for at least two days.

The student readily agreed.

The first night the royal couple gave him an uncomfortable bed in a small back room. They thought that if he was satisfied with such a bed, he could only be a student. If not, they thought, surely he must be a prince. A royal guard was stationed at the window to observe the student throughout the night.

As the young man undressed for the night, the dried peas spilled from his pockets onto the bed. He picked up as many as he could find, but as soon as he lay down, he felt another one and then another one and then another one beneath him. By daybreak he had gathered all the peas, but he had been up and down all night.

That morning the guard reported that the guest did not sleep but worked all night trying to make the bed comfortable. This confirmed the royal idea that he was accustomed to a luxurious bed. At breakfast, to be sure, the king asked him about his night's rest. Admitting that he had not slept well, the student said that it was his own fault but did not explain what had happened.

From this the king concluded that the young man was being gracious and did not want to put any blame on the palace for his sleepless night. He must indeed be a prince! From that time on he was treated like royalty.

That night the student slept in a royal bedroom in a royal bed. Having not slept the night before, he slept well. He had no trouble with the peas, because he had tied them in his handkerchief.

The next morning the guard reported that their guest had slept well all night. Now the royal couple was firmly convinced that he was a prince traveling incognito. Everyone was instructed to call him "Prince."

Convinced or not, the princess fell in love with him. He was so handsome and so courtly. He was not at all like the princes with whom she was familiar. She showered him with attention and in time they were married.

After one year of married bliss, the king ordered the royal carriages to take the royal couple to the prince's home country, so that the princess could see it and meet her parents-in-law. The royal groom was terrified. What if they learned the truth?

At first he stalled for time. That did not work. Then he decided, come what may, to begin the journey homeward. His plan was to desert the royal party and to return to the university if things went wrong. Just in case, he hid his student's uniform among his many belongings.

Far into the journey, they stopped in a forest for rest. Planning to run away, the make-believe prince wandered off and climbed down into a ditch to change his clothes. He discovered, to his amazement, that he was not alone. A seven-headed dragon was sleeping there.

"Who are you? What are you doing here?" asked the startled dragon.

The student told him his woes and his plan to escape.

"It isn't necessary for you to run away," said the dragon. "Just continue your journey. At the edge of the forest you will find a copper castle. Go to it and live there with your whole retinue. However, when the castle starts to move mysteriously and to rotate, you must leave immediately because I will come home. If I find you there, it will be your end."

Greatly relieved, he went back to his wife and retainers and continued the journey to the forest's edge. Sure enough, there was the copper castle, all ready to be occupied. They moved in and lived just as if they were at home.

For two years the couple lived comfortably and happily. Now, the make-believe prince thought, "I really am the ruler of a kingdom."

But one day the castle began moving mysteriously. In fact, it was rotating just as the dragon had said. Desperate, the young man went for a walk to think things through. On his way he met an old woman.

"What is wrong with Your Majesty?" she asked. "I can see from your furrowed brow that you have a great problem."

"Well, I am in great trouble," he said. Then he related his story to her.

"This is not too bad," said the old harridan. "You can be glad that you told your problem to me. I am queen of the witches and the fierce enemy of the seven-headed dragon. Now take my advice. Bake a loaf of bread and bake it seven times over. Put this bread at the castle gate. When the dragon comes, the bread will speak to him and ensure that he will never disturb you again. Then the castle will be yours forever."

"Thank you," said the prince. "It sounds strange to me, but I will do exactly as you have said."

Immediately he ordered his baker to prepare the dough according to instructions and bake the loaf seven times. After midnight he placed it at the castle gate.

At daybreak the dragon arrived. To his amazement, the bread called out to him, " I am the guard here and without my permission none can enter. If you want to come in, you have to endure everything I have endured."

"But this is my castle and I must enter," said the dragon. "What kinds of trials did you have to endure?"

"First, I was planted in the ground as grain and covered with dirt," the bread explained. "There I rotted, sprouted, and grew, all the while enduring cold, heat, rain, and snow until I produced a crop. After this I was cut, threshed, ground, and then kneaded into dough. Finally I was thrown seven times into a hot oven. If you can endure what I have endured, I will permit you to enter. Do you wish to try?" asked the bread.

The dragon knew that he could not endure what a simple loaf of bread had endured. He went into such a frustrated rage that he fell to the ground and died.

From then on the make-believe king became the real king of that country. After the deaths of his parents-in-law, he ruled over their country as well, making him the king of two countries. He is still ruling, if he has not died in the meantime.

Traveling students were often offered hospitality in palaces, and a handsome, well-mannered one could be mistaken for a prince traveling incognito. The concept of true or false royalty and the theme of the uncomfortable bed and peas is reminiscent of Hans Christian Andersen's story, "The Princess and the Pea" (1836).

This story was first collected and published by Kriza János in 1863 in the Szekler folklore compendium *Vadrózsák (Wild Roses)*. It originated in the former Háromszék County, present-day Covasna County, Romania. Kriza had started to collect the folktales of his hometown and its countryside in 1820, when he was merely a schoolboy. This famous folktale collector was born in 1811, studied theology and law in Kolozsvár (now Cluj-Napoca), and later studied in Berlin, Germany, where he became acquainted with the folktale collections of the Grimm brothers.

MILLIONS FOR AN EGG?

A*fter graduating from* the university at Pécs in Hungary, two friends began a tour of Europe. They traveled on foot because their resources were few, too few. Often they slept under the stars, but from time to time they longed for a bed and a good bath.

On one such occasion they spent the night at an inn named The Clever Goat. Here they had a meager breakfast, each eating a slice of bread and a single hard-boiled egg.

When it was time to pay, they had only enough money for the room. As they could not pay for breakfast, they were required to sign the debtors' record.

Sign they did and continued on their journey, never thinking again about the debt.

Years passed. One of the friends became a lawyer and the other a bishop. The bishop's ordination was widely publicized and the object of much talk because of its elegance.

Soon afterwards some travelers who spent the night in the

Clever Goat Inn discussed the ordination with the innkeeper. Because he often read the debtors' record to refresh his memory about who owed him money, the innkeeper recognized the name of the bishop. He was the young man who could not pay for his breakfast.

The innkeeper was now old, but he still wanted to collect the debt. This was surely his best opportunity. No bishop would want to be known as a debtor.

That evening he began to calculate: If that one egg the young man had eaten had hatched and produced a chick, this in turn would have produced more chicks, and they would have produced more chicks, and they would have produced even more chicks. His imagination carried him away. He calculated that in the previous twenty years that one egg would have produced enough chickens to feed all Hungary! In the end, the innkeeper calculated that the debt had grown to an enormous sum. He sent the bill to the bishop.

When the bishop refused to pay the bill, the innkeeper took the case to the court. The bishop thought that the judge and jury would see the absurdity of the bill, but he was wrong. The whole case seemed to be going against him, and the jailer was standing ready to take him to debtors' prison if he still refused to pay.

Just then his university friend, the lawyer, entered the courtroom, panting. Excusing himself for being late, the lawyer stated that he had come to defend the bishop.

"You may argue your case," said the judge, "but you have to have a very good reason for entering just as the case is being decided."

The lawyer began his presentation: "As soon as I heard about my friend's problem, I was ready to come to his defense. I was late, however, because I could not leave home until I planted some lentils left over from last night's supper."

The judge interrupted him: "Whoever heard of planting cooked lentils? Are you such a poor farmer that you don't know that cooked lentils will not produce a crop? You are speaking nonsense, and nonsense is not allowed in this courtroom."

"You are exactly right, Your Honor. That is my point and my whole argument in defense of the bishop. Cooked lentils cannot produce a crop, and a hard-boiled egg cannot produce a chick which can produce other chicks. The innkeeper's case is pure nonsense."

Caught in his own logic, the judge dismissed the case and admonished the bishop and the lawyer to pay for their long-ago breakfast.

Pay they did and left arm in arm, an old friendship renewed.

As an old proverb, that probably grew out of this story, says, "From hard-boiled eggs come no chicks."

During the seventeenth century the wandering of Hungarian students from university to university was particularly widespread. Famous schools were established at Debrecen, Sárospatak, Pápa, and Sopron and became the strongholds of Hungarian culture.

Bethlen Gábor, prince of Transylvania (1613–1629), cared especially for schools. He funded scholarships for Hungarian students at foreign universities and established a college and at least one academy.

Good education, however, did not always guarantee success in public life. Nimbleness of mind was absolutely indispensable for daily living, as many Hungarian folktales show.

THE FISH DAMSEL

Far, far away over the big sea lived an unhappy, poor widow. Her only joy was her son, who soon grew into a handsome young man.

It happened on a Sunday that they had no food in the house. It had so happened before, and it would so happen again. As usual, her son went to the sea with his fishing gear to catch some fish for their dinner. Catches were not so easy that day, because the sea was rougher than usual.

In time his patience paid off and he caught a small, shining fish. He rushed home to give it to his mother and then went back to try to catch another.

While she was waiting, his mother decided to clean the fish. She got her sharp knife and was ready to cut off the fish's head.

Suddenly the fish spoke. "Poor woman, don't kill me. I will do you and your son good if you spare me," said the fish.

"Oh," said the woman, "I have never heard of a talking fish. Of course I will spare you, but what will we eat for dinner?"

"I can help you," said the small, shiny fish. "First, put me to bed among the pillows. Then go to your son and wish as many fish as you want into his net."

She put the fish to bed among the pillows and hurried to her son. He was very surprised to see her. Then she told him about her conversation with the small, shiny fish.

"Let's see if it told the truth," said the young man. "How many fish shall we wish for?"

"For about a bucketful," his mother said. "Then I will choose the best ones, and we can throw the others back into the sea."

No sooner said than done. The net caught an exact bucketful of fish. The young man pulled it in, and his mother selected the fish she wanted. The others he threw back into the sea. Mother carried the fish in her apron and son carried his fishing gear home on his shoulder.

As soon as they opened the door, the small, shiny fish called out, "Dear Mother, are you pleased with me?"

"Yes, yes, my little fish," replied the mother. "I am very pleased with you, but now I have another problem. I don't have enough grease in which to fry so many fish."

"Dear Mother, just wish for as much as you want, but please hurry, because I'm getting hungry," said the small, shiny fish.

She wished to have her lard bucket full. No sooner had she wished than it began to fill. In fact, it filled exactly, not one drop less and not one drop more.

"Thank you, thank you, my little fish," she said.

Then glancing toward the bed, she saw the most beautiful young woman sitting there. The young woman stood up but said nothing.

The old widow and her son were astonished. The young man, in fact, immediately fell in love with the girl but could not utter even a word.

"Don't be surprised," said the fish damsel. "You have rescued me from a terrible curse. I will be your wife, and nought but death shall separate us. You may call the wedding guests at any time."

And call them he did.

When he returned, his mother asked him, "Whom did you invite, my dear son?"

"I invited the king and his noblemen," he said proudly.

"Now, then," said his mother, "you have not learned that it is not good to rub shoulders with the high and mighty. Why didn't you invite poor people such as we are? We have no space in this small hut to entertain nobility. Surely you will bring us to grief."

"I can solve the problem," said the fish damsel.

Thus saying, she went outside and, behold, a magic castle appeared.

At the appointed time the king and his noblemen arrived. As soon as the king saw the bride-to-be, he said to his noblemen, "Do whatever is necessary to persuade this young woman to marry me instead of this poor young man. I will have no rest until she is my wife."

"Your Majesty," they said, "tell the young man to come to the palace. Then order him to fell all the trees in the king's forest, cut and stack the wood, and dry it all in one day. Otherwise he will have it to pay."

The king followed their advice. When he heard this, the young man was very sad, because he knew that he had been given an impossible task.

When he arrived home, his bride-to-be noticed his sadness and asked why he was so dejected.

"I am in great trouble," he said. "The king has given me an impossible task upon peril of my life. I am afraid that death shall soon part us."

"Tell me what your task is," she said. "I think that I can help you."

"The king has ordered me to fell all the trees in the royal forest, cut and stack the wood, and dry it all in one day," he said.

"Your mother was right," she said. "It is not good to rub shoulders with the high and mighty. It is certain that the king wants you out of the way so that he can take me for his wife. We will fool him, because I can do something about this. Now let us each go to bed and get a good night's sleep. We shall see what the morning will bring."

Then she stepped out into the yard and blew a silver whistle. Soon the yard was filled with forest spirits, to whom she gave orders to fell all the trees in the king's forest, cut and stack the wood, and to dry it, all before morning.

The next morning the king looked out of his castle window

toward his forest. To his amazement it was not there. Instead, there were only piles and piles of cut, stacked, and dry wood. Calling his noblemen, the king rebuked them sharply.

"This time we are sure to succeed," said the noblemen. "Give him orders to remove the mountain behind the palace and to turn the place into a vineyard with grapes, all by tomorrow morning."

No sooner said than done.

Again the young man returned home dejected.

"Ah, what problems we have for having rubbed shoulders with the high and mighty," sighed his bride-to-be. "Yet I am sure that I can do something about this, too. Let us go to the mountain."

Once there she blew her silver whistle again. Instantly they were surrounded by mountain spirits, to whom she gave orders to remove the mountain and to turn the place into a vineyard with grapes.

No sooner said than done.

In the morning the king looked out of his castle window toward the mountain. To his amazement it was not there. In its place was a beautiful vineyard brimming with large, ripe grapes. Now he had no beautiful forest, no beautiful mountain, and no beautiful wife. How unhappy he was!

Rebuking his noblemen a second time, he demanded a plan which was sure to succeed.

"Your Majesty," they said. "Already he has done two impossible things, but we know one which he cannot do. Send the young man to invite the Spirit of Heaven and Earth for dinner tomorrow."

The young man was now more than dejected. He was in shock and returned home with his head bowed.

Seeing him in this condition, his bride-to-be asked, "What is it this time?"

"I must invite the Spirit of Heaven and Earth to have dinner with the king tomorrow," he said.

"Ah," she sighed again, "what problems we have for having rubbed shoulders with the high and mighty. Now do what I tell you. Mount your horse, and let it go where it pleases and stop where it pleases."

He mounted his horse, and to his surprise it became a magnificent steed, sprouted wings, and flew and flew and flew until it stopped at the abode of the Spirit of Heaven and Earth.

Then a voice thundered forth: "Poor young man, I know why you have come. Go home with a happy heart. Tomorrow as you are going to the palace, I will repay the king and his noblemen for all the evil they have done."

Ordering the winged horse to return home, the young man found himself immediately beside his bride-to-be and his horse standing in its usual place.

Early in the morning he left for the palace, and when it was in view, the heavens became utterly dark, he heard a mighty peal of thunder and saw a blinding flash of lightning . Then he heard the now-familiar rumbling voice, "Look toward the palace."

Suddenly it was as light as it had been dark. The young man could not believe his eyes. In place of the palace was a large pond surrounded with courtly robes and filled with frogs.

Again the voice came from above. "The frogs are the king

and his noblemen. Every conceited, malicious, high and mighty man will come to grief and nought. And you. You must learn who you are and where you belong. Be not proud; be not eager to be more than you are."

With these words the Spirit of Heaven and Earth returned to his place, wherever it is. The young man, too, returned to his place, a little older and a lot wiser.

From then on the young couple lived happily together. In fact, they are still living that way, if they have not died in the meantime.

A morality story, this centers on the idea that the supernatural, whatever it is, is on the side of good and against evil. Between its traditional Hungarian beginning and ending, magic rules, but the message is clear: "You must learn who you are and where you belong." Such a cautionary tale could be a sign of a society in transition, in which the aristocrats have become too overbearing, and the poor people uncertain of their place in a changing world.

As in many folktales, a woman is the central figure and heroine.

TALKING GRAPES, SMILING APPLES, AND RINGING APRICOTS

SeveN *times seventy-seven years ago* the king of Cloud-Cuckoo-Land decided to take a journey around the world. He called his three daughters, Sarolta, Gizella, and Ilona, and told them, "I will leave for a long journey before the first cuckoo call. I hope to spend some time at the palace of your fairy-queen godmother. I will bring home a beautiful present for each of you, so please tell me what you would like."

Sarolta said, "Please get me the funniest animal you can find."

Gizella said, "Please get me a golden tambourine which can play the music of the spheres."

Ilona was silent, so her father asked her again, "And you, my darling daughter, what would you like for me to bring you? Surely you would like something."

Ilona thought for awhile and then said quietly, "I would like to have talking grapes, smiling apples, and ringing apricots."

He promised to bring them what they had requested. He knew that their godmother would help him. What would be difficult for him would be easy for her. After all, she was the fairy queen. Little did he know that many cuckoo nestlings would leave their nests before his return.

Finding the gifts became the crowning object of his trip. First, he found a trained, talking monkey for Sarolta. Then he found tambourines which could play the music of the spheres for Gizella.

"So far, so good," he thought to himself. "Now I must visit their godmother. Once I find the gift for Ilona, I will be free to take in the rest of the world."

Arriving at her castle, he told the fairy queen his mission. "I will help you," she said, "but it will not be easy, not even for me. I can hardly imagine such things as talking grapes, smiling apples, and ringing apricots. Surely they exist somewhere other than in the land of make-believe. If they do, we will find them. Tomorrow we will begin our search."

Begin they did. They went from one fair to another, asking everyone they met about the sought-after gifts. No one had ever heard of them.

After weeks of searching, they decided that the youngest princess would have to settle for something else. The king turned his carriage toward the fairy queen's castle. The horses galloped so fast that they seemed almost to fly, but the road took them through marshland. Both horses and carriage were soon hopelessly bogged down in deep mud.

Summoning the help of all strong men nearby, the king

hoped to be soon on the way. Despite their best efforts, the carriage remained stuck fast, and the men went home covered with mud.

Toward evening a large boar approached the carriage. Although the king was not easily amazed, he was when the boar began to speak with a very cultured voice: "I will push your carriage out of the mud if you will give me your youngest daughter in marriage."

Desperate and thinking the marriage of a boar with a young woman among the most ridiculous things he had ever heard, the king promised to meet the boar's condition.

Putting his big snout against one of the wheels, the boar pushed and pushed until the carriage was once again on solid ground. Off the horses galloped so fast that they almost flew. In no time, the king left the fairy queen at her castle and continued his journey home.

"East or west," he kept saying to himself, "home is best."

In due time the palace guard announced the safe arrival of the royal carriage. What joy there was in the palace at the news! The three princesses ran to the gate.

While they were hugging their father, a monkey sprang out of the carriage and turned cartwheels as he presented himself to Sarolta, saying, "I am a gift in a gaudy suit, and the bow is right here under my chin."

Then—seemingly out of nowhere—there came the most heavenly music. The king presented the tambourines to Gizella. She was entranced by their harmonies.

As was her quiet nature, Ilona waited patiently for her

gift, but there was none. Her father told her of his quest and of his failure to find talking grapes, smiling apples, and ringing apricots. For her it was enough that her beloved father was home.

At dinner the king told his daughters about his misfortune in the marshland and about his promise to the boar. Assuring Ilona that he had no intention of giving her in marriage to a boar, he excused himself to prepare for a good night's sleep.

The next morning a loud cuckoo call awakened the royal family. A herald reported that a strange visitor had removed the gate from its pillars and had entered the reception hall. The stranger demanded to see the king.

The king suspected the identity of the uninvited visitor and was in no hurry to go to meet him. When he entered the reception hall, he found the boar spotlessly clean, seated, and waiting.

"My name is Adalbert, Swine Prince of the Marshlands," he announced. "I have come to claim my bride."

"I gave you my word," said the king. "I will go and bring her to you."

Upon leaving the hall, he ordered that an attractive servant girl be dressed in one of Ilona's beautiful gowns and presented to the swine prince as his bride.

When the maid was ushered in, the swine prince cried out, "Why are you trying to deceive me? I know the difference between a princess and an ordinary young woman in royal dress." With this he stormed out.

After several more days he appeared again at the palace and demanded his bride. The king had already planned his next move. He brought in Ilona dressed as a peasant girl.

But Adalbert saw through the ruse. "Now you have kept your promise," he said. "Come, my bride; let us be going."

The king tried to make excuses, but none availed. The king's word was the king's word. If it was not good, all honesty would be lost from the land.

Ilona spoke quietly to her father: "Your Majesty, you have to keep your promise, and I have to keep my wits about me to outwit wizards, dragons, and even this bold beast."

With these words she climbed into the saddle on the swine prince's back and they were gone. He ran over hill and dale until at sunset they reached a shanty in the marsh.

"This is my palace," he said. "Here you can sleep on some fresh straw and eat some cornbread for supper."

Weary from the journey, the princess fell asleep on her straw bed. When she awakened in the morning, she did not recognize where she was. The couch on which she lay was pure gold, the quilts and pillows of pure silk, and the walls were covered with fine leather. There were pigs-in-waiting to do her bidding and a royal gown for her to wear. When she entered the dining hall, the swine prince was seated at the head of the table eating some golden corn.

After breakfast he introduced the royal herd to Ilona and gave her these instructions: "Take care of my seventy-seven golden piglets. Watch their diet, which is one cup of golden corn for breakfast each day. Then let them rove in the orchard and feed on the fruit that falls from the trees.

"Stay away from the royal pig wallow, but go to the hot springs to let them bathe every evening. Otherwise the palace will be turned into a pigsty. After a time, shorter or longer, I will return from a journey which I must take."

Ilona understood his instructions and said, "I will discipline the golden piglets with a magic whip made from one of my golden braids."

Then he left without telling anyone where he was going or when he would be back. His servants speculated, but no one knew for sure.

After many days the swine prince returned, pushing a barrel ahead of him with his powerful snout. He emptied its contents into the royal pig wallow and then jumped in himself. There he wallowed all night.

In the morning Ilona was awakened by a louder-than-usual grunt coming from the pig wallow. She saw Adalbert struggling with all his strength to get out of the wallow, but he was stuck tight. Then, with a mighty twist he wrenched free, leaving his pig skin behind. What emerged from the wallow was a handsome prince! For years he and his retainers had dwelled in the swamp as swine, cursed by a witch for foiling her schemes of wickedness. But now, the curse was gone!

The golden piglets ran squealing and jumped into the mud. They wallowed and wallowed until they, too, had shed their skins and emerged as soldiers of the royal guard.

That very same day the royal messengers sped out to deliver the wedding invitations. Then Prince Adalbert took Ilona into one of his orchards, where he gave his bride-to-be wedding gifts: talking grapes, smiling apples, and ringing apricots.

Many fairy tales and magic stories originate in Byzantine sources. This story is an excellent example of cross-cultural fertilization with the Ottoman Turks who occupied Hungary from 1541 to 1686. A Turkish version of this story, "The Princess and the Pig," appears in *A Treasury of Turkish Folktales for Children* by Barbara K. Walker (Linnet, 1988).

This tale offers a veritable feast of folktale incidents and ingredients, including the transformation of a prince into a beast, a virtuous princess, and a fairy godmother. The setting in "Cloud-Cuckoo-Land" reveals that this story is a fantasy.

To Outwit a Count

When *Count Bánfy* celebrated his fiftieth birthday, he invited a mansion full of guests: counts and countesses, princes and princesses, barons and baronesses from far and near. He did not, however, invite the poor families who worked on his estate.

Jóska was no ordinary farmhand. He had a brain and he was clever. Also, he wanted desperately to crash the count's birthday celebration. The wealthy guests were sure to have pity on him and his large family, he thought. Maybe they would give him money.

From somewhere Jóska got a fat goose. It may have been from the count's own farmyard. No one will ever know. He took it to his wife and asked her to roast it to a golden brown and to put it on their best platter.

After some hours of preparation, Jóska left for the mansion with the goose on the platter. When he showed his gift to the gatekeepers, he had little trouble getting past them. Admission to the banquet hall was a little harder, but he succeeded. He had often worked for the count in the mansion and knew every centimeter of it by heart.

Jóska walked boldly to the count's head table with the goose held out before him and announced, "May you live a hundred and twenty years! Please accept a gift from my family."

The count was astonished but soon regained his composure. Jóska was one of his favorites among the workers on his estate, and he had come to expect almost anything except bad from him. The guests were even more astonished!

"Thank you, Jóska," he said. "I know you are clever, so I want to propose a riddle to you for the sake of my guests. Here it is: How are the six members of my family to share this fine goose equally? What is your solution?"

With eyes twinkling, Jóska looked straight at the count and said, "The solution is simple. Sir, you are the head of the family, so you get the head of the goose. The countess is right behind you, so she gets the neck. The two young countesses will soon marry and fly from the family nest, so they get the two wings. The two young counts will soon be old enough to stand on their own two feet, so they get the feet."

"And what will happen to the rest?" asked the count.

"Sir, you are a very generous man and will allow me to take what is left to my many children. They have never eaten goose before."

The count smiled knowingly, and all his guests were in high spirits. In fact, they took a collection for Jóska and his family, and he left with the goose and seventy-seven gold coins.

The news spread quickly among the other families. Not to be outdone, Gábor got five geese from somewhere and asked his wife to roast them just as Jóska's wife had done. He calculated that for five geese he would receive five times the amount Jóska received.

He, too, gained entry to the banquet hall. Going directly to the count, he said, "May you live a hundred and twenty years! Please accept a gift from my family."

"Thank you, Gábor," said the count. "Now I will propose a riddle to you for the sake of my guests. How are the six members of my family to share the five geese equally?

"I am sorry, sir. I have no solution for such a problem. Someone from your kitchen staff will have to answer it," said Gábor.

The dinner guests were on the edges of their seats. They suggested calling Jóska to solve the riddle. The count acquiesced and Jóska was called. He came running.

The count told him, "Now you have a more difficult riddle. Here are five geese. How are we to divide them equally among the six members of my family?"

"My lord, that is a trifle. My lord and my lady and one goose make three. The two young countesses and one goose make three. The two young counts and one goose make three, and I and two geese also make three," said Jóska.

At this the count gave Jóska one hundred gold pieces. Following the example of their host, the guests matched his generosity.

On his way home Jóska left one roasted goose and some gold pieces with Gábor and his family. His eyes twinkled, his smile extended from ear to ear, and his song reached the ears of all the farmworkers in their little settlement.

This story is deeply rooted in Hungarian soil. Nobility and clever peasants are stock characters in Hungarian folktales. A count was a high-ranking nobleman, owner of huge landed estates, the governor of a county in a feudal state.

A roasted goose was a welcome gift on any occasion. Goose was and is dear to the Hungarian stomach. In fact, Hungary today produces more goose liver pâté than even France.

This tale, with a number of variations, was known from Russia to Germany. For example, in the German version the fowl are quail instead of geese.

A Poor Man's Bargain

In a village far beyond the seven seas lived a poor man with rich neighbors on both sides. The two rich men were almost wallowing in land, livestock, and money. The poor man had only a gaunt cow.

On a Friday morning the two rich neighbors set out for the market to sell some fine oxen. Upon seeing them, the poor man's wife, Zsófi, said to her husband, "Lajos, you ought to go to the market, too. Maybe you could sell our cow, but don't sell her unless the buyer is willing to buy you a drink to seal the deal."

When the poor man went out the gate with the gaunt cow, he could see his neighbors and their fine oxen far ahead of him. He was more than willing to keep the distance between them.

As he neared the market, the road became crowded with

people and animals. A man with a goat came up alongside Lajos and said, "My goat is almost as big as your cow. Would you like to trade?"

"Yes, I'm willing to trade my cow for your goat, but you have to buy me a drink to seal the deal," he said.

Soon they were gulping down their drinks, and then the poor man went on his way toward the market with his newly acquired goat. Upon entering, he found a place among the sellers of animals. The man standing beside him had a fat goose. He said to Lajos, "You see what a fine, fat goose I have? Would you like to trade?"

"Yes, I'm willing to trade my goat for your goose, but you have to buy me a drink to seal the deal," he said.

Soon they were gulping down their drinks, and then the poor man went back to his place to sell his fine, fat goose. This time the man beside him had a bright red rooster, which crowed loudly. The man said to Lajos, "You see what a fine red rooster I have? He crows at just the right time each morning so that no one oversleeps. Would you like to trade?"

"Yes, I'm willing to trade my goose for your rooster, but you have to buy me a drink to seal the deal," he said.

Soon they were gulping down their drinks, and then the poor man went back to his place with his red rooster under his arm. While he was waiting, some old friends stopped to chat. "It is lunchtime," said one. "Wouldn't you like to eat with us?"

"Yes, I'm willing to eat with you, but you have to buy me a drink to go with my lunch," he said.

"What shall we eat?" asked one. "We have here only a bottle of good wine and some bread."

Another said, "Some fried chicken would go very well with bread and wine. What do you say, my friend?"

Not wanting to deny his friends, Lajos agreed and butchered the rooster. In a short time it was fried and eaten. Wiping their mouths with the backs of their hands, the friends thanked him for the fried chicken and stood up to leave.

At this the poor man said, "This is not right, my friends. I came here with a cow, exchanged it for a goat, which I exchanged for a fine, fat goose, which I exchanged for the rooster, which we have just eaten. How can I go home empty-handed to my wife? What will my neighbors say?"

"We'll see what we have in our bags," they said. "Whatever is there is yours."

When they looked, they found that they had only two onions, which they gave to the poor man. Then all left for home.

On his way the poor man met his rich neighbors, who had not succeeded in selling their oxen. They asked, "Where is your cow, Lajos?"

"I traded it for a goat," he said.

"And where is the goat?" they asked.

"I traded it for a fine, fat goose."

"And where is the fine, fat goose?"

I traded it for a bright red rooster which crowed at the right time in the morning."

"And where is the bright red rooster?"

"Some friends saw me at the market, and at lunchtime they persuaded me to butcher the rooster so that we could have fried chicken for lunch."

"And what will your wife say when you get home with nothing?"

"But I have something," he said. "See, here are two onions which I received from my friends."

The neighbors laughed and said, "It is sure that your wife will chase you out of the house. You will be the laughingstock of the whole village. Whoever heard of a husband's doing what you have done?"

"No," he said. "My wife won't even scold me. I am sure."

"We will make you a bet," they said. "If your wife scolds you, we get your house and garden. If she doesn't, you get these twelve oxen. Is it a wager?"

"It is," he said. "I agree, but let's put it in writing."

Put it in writing they did. Neighbors who were also on their way home signed it as witnesses, and all continued on their way.

Lajos arrived home, and the neighbors ran to the window of his house to overhear the conversation. Zsófi welcomed him with a big hug and kiss and then asked, "Did you make a good bargain?"

"Yes, I did," he said.

"And did you seal the bargain with a drink?" she asked.

"Yes, I did."

"How much did you receive for the cow?"

"I traded it for a goat."

"You did well," she said, "because we need goat milk."

"But I traded the goat for a fine, fat goose."

"And did you seal the bargain with a drink?"

"Yes, I did."

"You did well," she said, "because we need feathers to make a pillow."

"But I traded the fine, fat goose for a bright red rooster which crowed at the right time in the morning."

"And did you seal the bargain with a drink?"

"Yes, I did."

"You did well," she said, "because we have no clock and the rooster will awaken us at the right time in the morning."

"But I have no rooster. Some of my friends saw me at lunchtime and persuaded me to butcher the rooster so that we could have fried chicken with their bread and wine."

"You did well," she said, "because it would not have been good for you to stand at the market all day without having eaten. Did you bring me anything from the market?"

"Look, here in my bag are two onions."

"You did well," she said, "because now our rich neighbors can't sneer at us and say that we don't even have an onion."

Amazed at the conversation, the neighbors came to the door with their oxen and paid their debt. The poor man's last bargain was his best.

Fairs were the biggest commercial and social events of the year in Hungary. St. Martin's Day fair in the first part of November was the most important Transylvanian fair. This was a seasonal gathering, where buyers and sellers met together. Farm products and animals were the prime commodities.

Everyone was looking for a bargain or at least for entertainment. There was no shortage of amusements, such as circus performances, merry-go-rounds, and outdoor cooking, called *lacikonyha*. People who would otherwise rarely leave their villages would venture out once a year to St. Martin's Day fair.

Marci, the Honest Thief

Long ago and far away lived a poor woman. She had a son, Marci, an honest and upright boy. He was also skillful, quick-witted, and well known in those parts for his common sense.

The king heard about his reputation and became envious. He was afraid that his own reputation for practical wisdom would be overshadowed by that of Marci, so he called the boy to court for the sole purpose of outsmarting him.

"Are you the Marci who is so well known for common sense?" asked the king. "Are you really as bright as I have heard that you are? I want you to prove it to me. If you know so much, do you know how to steal?"

"Your Majesty," replied Marci, "I have never stolen in my whole life. God helping me, I never will."

"Ah," said the king, "but you must. That you have never stolen means nothing to me. I have twelve plowmen working in my field. You must steal the twelve yoke of oxen and the twelve plows from them upon peril of your life. If you succeed, you will become their rightful owner."

Marci went home with a heavy heart and told his mother about the king's demands.

"Just think about it," said his mother. "You are sure to find a solution."

Think about it he did, and in a few days he said to his mother, "For my plan I need a mother hen and twelve black chicks."

"What do you want with them?" she asked, but she received no answer. She got the mother hen and twelve black chicks and gave them to him.

Marci left immediately for the edge of the forest next to the field where the twelve plowmen were plowing with their twelve yoke of oxen and their twelve plows. There he released the birds and shouted, "Look! A wild hen and her twelve chicks! Catch them, and they will bring you good luck!"

The twelve plowmen left their twelve yoke of oxen and twelve plows and rushed into the forest to catch the hen and her chicks. Marci quickly stole the twelve yoke of oxen and the twelve plows and took them home.

When he sent his mother to the king to announce that he was now the proud owner of twelve yoke of oxen and twelve plows, the king became very angry and called for Marci a second time. "So you succeeded, did you?" said the king.

"Yes, Your Majesty," replied Marci.

"You were lucky. Anyone can steal something if it is unguarded. Now you must steal the wheat from my granary. It is heavily guarded day and night. You have only until tomorrow morning to do this upon peril of your life," said the king.

Again Marci left with a heavy heart. He had to steal against his wishes and his life was in peril. What could he possibly do?

To make it more difficult, the king doubled the guard and ordered them to do their worst when Marci appeared.

Marci, however, learned about the king's order and devised a plan. He made a straw man, dressed it in his own clothes, and put his own cap on its head. Toward dark he stealthily placed it in front of the granary. Then he hid himself and sneezed loudly.

Guards seemed to come from everywhere. They saw the straw man right at the door and attacked. One severed its head, and the others did their worst. Nothing remained except a pile of cut-up clothes and straw.

Convinced that they had done their job, the guards went to the king to report their success. He was overjoyed and feted them with the best of his food and wine.

In the meantime, Marci stole the wheat and again sent his mother to the king to report his success.

The king was blue with rage and rushed to the granary to investigate. He found it exactly as Marci reported and ordered the guards who were so readily deceived to be put to death.

A third time the king called Marci to the palace. "So you succeeded, did you?" shouted the king.

"Yes, Your Majesty," replied Marci.

"You were lucky again," said the king. "The guards were

only fools. Now I have a real test for you. You must steal my golden-haired steed from the royal stable. It is guarded at all times by one hundred armed stablemen. If you succeed, my crown is yours. If not, your head is mine."

"It would be more equitable, sir, if it were your head or mine," said Marci. "Be it as it may, I have to try."

To make it more difficult, the king doubled the guard and ordered them to do their worst when Marci appeared.

Again Marci heard of the king's order. It was not intended to be secret. It was intended to be a discouragement.

This time his heart was not heavy. He already had a plan. He bought several bottles of brandy and put sleeping potion in them. Then he put on the shabby clothes of a drunkard. In the evening toward dark he rattled the stable door.

Knowing what had happened to the guards at the granary, the stablemen were not eager to admit even a drunkard. However, when they saw that he had several bottles of brandy, they let him in and, when he appeared to fall asleep on a pile of straw, they drank his brandy. One by one they fell asleep, even the ones holding the reins and the tail of the king's steed and the one mounted in the saddle on its back. When all were asleep, Marci led the horse to his own barn.

In the morning the king went personally to the royal stable. Shocked, he found the horse missing and all the stablemen sleeping soundly.

Unable to give any reasonable account for being deceived, they, too, met their untimely ends. The king decided that only he was competent to stand guard when he gave Marci an assignment.

This time Marci did not send his mother. He went directly to the king and claimed the kingly crown.

"So you succeeded, did you?" raged the king. "You were lucky. Again the guards were only so many fools. Now I myself will stand guard and we will see how lucky you are. Now you must steal my dinner tomorrow. If you succeed, you will receive my sword. If not, I will receive your head."

This time Marci made a wooden hand and put it on a stick, to which he fastened a rope. He made a small opening under the royal kitchen window in line with the cook's table.

The next day when the king was sitting in the dining hall and the butler was about to serve, Marci pushed the hand through the hole and guided it toward the royal platter. When the butler saw it, he ran from the kitchen to the king and reported that Marci was trying to steal his dinner. Grabbing his sword, the king sprang to the kitchen and cut the hand off its wooden arm. Marci pulled on the rope, withdrew the stick, and raced for the palace door. The king, wanting to finish the job, burst out the kitchen door looking for the bleeding Marci. While he was outside, Marci was inside stealing his royal dinner.

Again, Marci went to the king and this time claimed the royal sword.

"So you succeeded, did you?" snarled the king. "You are a very lucky young man. Even a king can be fooled once, but not a second time."

"Your Majesty," said Marci, "your servants were given only one opportunity. Shouldn't you meet an untimely end yourself for being deceived?"

"But I am the king!" he shouted. "They were only ordinary men. I am worth a million of them. I have one more test for you. If you succeed, I will give you the princess in marriage. If not, I will receive your head. This is the test: You must steal the golden ring from the queen's finger before morning."

Towards evening Marci sneaked into the royal suite in the palace and heard the king say to his wife, "My dear, I'm going to take a short walk. When I return, I want you to give me your golden ring for safekeeping. That rascally Marci will try to steal it tonight."

As soon as the king left, Marci quietly entered the royal bedchamber and waited until the queen had gone to bed. Then, disguising his voice, he said, "My dear, I'm back. Now give me the ring."

Half-asleep, the queen handed him the ring in the gathering darkness. Marci remained hidden behind the door. When the king came in and began to light a candle, he sneaked out as quietly as he had come in.

In the candlelight, the king sat down beside the sleeping queen and said softly, "I have returned, my dear. Now please give me your golden ring for safekeeping until morning."

Half-awake, half-asleep, the queen replied, "Don't you remember, my love, that I gave the ring to you only a few minutes ago? You asked for it, and I put it into your hand. Now come to bed and think no more of this until morning."

Sleep he could not. His rage was so great that the king could not contain himself. He sat at a table drinking a bottle of Tokay wine until it and the night were gone.

As the king expected, Marci appeared in the morning with

the golden ring in hand to claim the princess for his bride. She was famed for beauty and intelligence and was the object of countless royal and wealthy suitors.

Coming to his senses at last and recognizing defeat, the king said quietly, "So you succeeded again, did you? You alone are worthy of the princess. Come, my son. You will make a deserving successor to the throne when I am gone."

The wedding celebration lasted a whole week. Never before and never after was there such a wedding. Nobles and commoners from far and near streamed through the palace grounds and ate and drank to their hearts' content. The Gypsy musicians played their fiddles, sang, and danced. They are still playing, singing, and dancing, if they haven't died in the meantime.

Nineteenth century folklore and Hungarian literature abound in outlaw-like characters, called *betyár*. Marci was not a real outlaw, but he is forced into actions that qualify him as one of those plucky fellows.

The violent recruiting of soldiers by the Hapsburgs between 1715 and 1807 forced many poor young men to choose a life of theft to avoid serving in the emperor's army. The freedom-loving outlaws always enjoyed the sympathy of the oppressed, poor people.

Rózsa Sándor and Sobri Jóska were the best known Hungarian outlaws. Rózsa and his band served as a valiant cavalry troop and fought bravely in the 1848 Hungarian War of Independence. Their weapon was the short-stocked long whip of Hungarian herdsmen. After this war, the age of the outlaws was over.

This folktale is found in several cultures under various titles. In the Grimms' complete collection it is known as "The Master Thief."

The Strongest Creature

A *bear and a wolf* lived in the same forest. One year the drought was so severe that they could hardly find food. Both of them planned to visit the village's sheepfolds and barns.

One day the bear met the wolf and said, "Good morning, my friend wolf."

The wolf replied, "For me it's not a good morning. Even if you wish it for me, it won't be good. Anyway, thank you."

The bear asked, "Is something wrong with you?"

The wolf replied, "Don't ask me. Trouble! I've had trouble, and I will have more of it."

The bear asked again, "Are you hungry? You look as thin as a dragonfly."

The wolf just sighed, "That is one trouble, but it is not the only one. There are others."

The bear observed the wolf carefully and, noticing that his fur was torn, asked, "Did you fight with one of your relatives?"

Waving his paw in resignation, he said, "No. I fought with a man."

Smiling, the bear asked, "Only with a man?"

The wolf was surprised. "Only with a man? Surely there is no stronger creature than a man!"

Suspecting that something bad had happened, the bear said, "Tell me what is the matter."

The wolf, looking around cautiously, said, "I couldn't endure the hunger any longer, so I sneaked into the village to steal a fat lamb or a piglet. I was careful, but the dogs smelled me and began barking at the top of their lungs. A man ran up to me and began hitting me with something so badly that I could hardly drag myself away. I was lucky that the dogs did not tear me apart, because I could not have escaped from them."

In disbelief the bear said again, "A man! He is a weakling. He is only a man. I have beaten him and eaten him many times."

"Believe me," said the wolf. "There is no stronger creature than a man. Before you were lucky. Some day you, too, will learn what I have learned."

The bear straightened up with pride and said, "I will show you. The next time I meet a man I will tear him to pieces as quickly as I could this shrub."

"It's easy to be brave with a shrub, but a man is not a shrub. I don't know what you will be able to do with the next man you meet," said the wolf.

"Well, I know," said the bear conceitedly. "I will eat him and spit out the bones."

"Oh, tell that to a horse," said the wolf. "I know from experience."

"Let's bet on it. I bet you a fat rabbit," said the bear with great confidence.

"If you can still find a fat rabbit," said the wolf, agreeing to the bet.

They went together to the edge of the forest just outside the village and lay in ambush by the village road. There was no other. They waited and waited.

Finally a child passed by.

"This is only a child," said the wolf. "Our bet is about a man. We still have some waiting to do."

Then an old beggar passed by.

"This one does not count either. The child will someday be a man, and this beggar was once a man. We must wait for a real man."

After some more waiting, a young woman walked toward the village.

Again the wolf spoke, "This is not a man either. This is only the wife or daughter of a man. We must wait for a man or the bet is no good. I would not give you a fat rabbit for a child or an old beggar or a woman. Only a man is worth a fat rabbit."

Finally a man dressed in a uniform appeared on the road. He was, in fact, a soldier in the regiment which protected the village.

"Does this man count?" asked the bear. "He looks as manly as a man can look."

"Yes, this is a real man," said the wolf. "Now let's see what you can do. As for me, I am running back into the woods as fast as I can. I learned well from my experience."

The bear rushed right into the middle of the road and roared ferociously with his mouth wide open and his powerful limbs flailing menacingly.

At once the soldier stood his ground and fired several shots directly at the bear. Failing to frighten the bear into retreat, he took out his sword and slashed the bear several times.

All the time the bear could not get close enough to do any damage at all. Seeing that the situation was only going to get worse, he fled over hedge and ditch into the forest.

Later, after his wounds had healed somewhat, the bear met the wolf again. "I guess that I owe you a fat rabbit," he said. "You were right about a man's being the strongest of the creatures. That man was not like any other man I ever encountered."

"Tell me what happened. It looks like you came out the worse for your meeting that man," said the wolf.

"I tell you the truth. Never in my life have I seen a creature as strange as that man," said the bear sheepishly. "When I wanted to attack him on the road, I moved toward him growling menacingly. He never budged at all. Instead, he spit something that hit me so hard that I saw stars. Still I moved closer, but he still stood his ground. Then he stuck out what seemed to be a shiny tongue and slashed my thick fur right to what little meat remains on me. I was in real danger of losing my life. Frightened and ashamed, I retreated from the battlefield into the woods. Like you, I have learned my lesson. I am just lucky to be alive."

In this story we meet with a stock character of Hungarian folktales, the Hussar. These soldiers were typical Hungarian light cavalry who emerged in the army of Bethlen Gábor, prince of Transylvania (1613–1629). They were the most successful fighters on the international battlefields of the Thirty Years' War, when Bethlen opposed the Holy Roman Emperor. The Hussars also distinguished themselves during the wars against the Ottoman Turks.

THE FOX, THE BEAR, AND THE POOR MAN

A *very long time ago* a poor man went out to plow a field with his cow. When he passed by the forest, he heard some roaring and squealing. He was curious, so he walked into the forest to see what was going on. There he saw a bear trying to catch a rabbit.

"I've never seen anything like this," he said and laughed until he almost burst his sides.

"How dare you laugh at me?" bawled the bear. "You'll have to pay for this. I will eat both you and your cow."

That ended the poor man's laughing. He pleaded with the bear to wait until evening so that he could first plow his field. He did not want to leave his family without bread.

"O.K., I'll leave you alone until evening, but then I will eat you," said the bear, and back he went to chasing the rabbit.

The poor man was desperate as he plowed. All he could think about was how to placate the bear and save his life.

The Fox, the Bear, and the Poor Man

At about lunchtime, a fox came by and, noticing that the man was very sad, asked, "What is your problem? Perhaps I can help you."

At this the man told him about his encounter with the bear.

"That is not a very difficult problem. I can help you to stay as fit as a fiddle. What will you pay me for my help?" asked the fox.

The poor man did not know what to promise. He owned almost nothing, and knowing foxes, he knew that the fox wanted a lot. Finally they agreed on nine fat hens and one rooster. The problem was that the man did not have money to buy them.

"O.K., poor man. Listen to me," said the fox. "Towards evening when the bear comes, I will hide myself in the bushes and blow the hunting horn. When the bear asks about it, you will say that hunters are coming to your rescue. The bear will be frightened and will beg you to hide him. You hide him in that big coal sack and tell him not to budge. Then I will come out of the bush, pretending to be a hunter, and ask you what you have in the sack. You will say that you have only some coal. Then I will say that I will not believe it unless you strike your ax into it. So you will strike the bear dead."

Everything went exactly as planned. The bear got the worst of it, and the man and his cow escaped being his supper.

"Didn't I tell you that all is well which ends well?" bragged the fox. "Now I have some other business to do. Tomorrow I will come for the nine fat hens and the one rooster. Stay home and wait for me. Otherwise you will come to grief."

The poor man loaded the bear into his wagon and went happily home. He prepared a good dinner of bear meat, ate well, and slept like a log. He wasn't afraid of the fox, because he had learned to use his brain. What was bad for the bear would be bad for the fox.

Early in the morning the fox knocked at the door and demanded the nine fat hens and one rooster.

"Just a few minutes, my friend. Let me get dressed," called the man.

Get dressed he did, but he didn't open the door. Instead he began to bark like a foxhound.

"Hey, poor man! What is that? Isn't it the barking of a foxhound?" asked the fox.

"Yes, my friend, two foxhounds are here. They caught your scent on my clothes when I entered the village yesterday evening and have slept the night under my bed. Now they have caught your scent again, so I dare not open the door or they will tear you to pieces. You saved my life, so it is the least that I can do to save yours," the poor man replied.

"Thank you! Please keep them inside until I am at a distance. What good will nine fat hens and a rooster do me if the hounds tear me to shreds? Goodbye, my friend! Perhaps we will meet again under happier circumstances," shouted the fox as he fled.

When the poor man opened the door, the fox was no more to be seen. He just laughed and laughed until he almost burst his sides. Maybe he is still laughing, if he hasn't died in the meantime.

THE FOX, THE BEAR, AND THE POOR MAN

This poor man might have been a serf, plowing the land of the liege lord. Hungary was organized as a feudal state during the reigns of (St.) Ladislaus I (1077–1095) and Kálmán (the Bookish) 1095–1116. Lords possessed huge landed estates, and often the serfs of twenty to thirty villages worked for one lord. The serfs were bound to the soil, being subject to the will of their lords. The increasing bitterness of the serfs led to peasant revolts which significantly shook the bases of feudalism in Hungary in the fifteenth and sixteenth centuries.

Twelve at a Swat

Once upon a time lived a Gypsy family. The father had as many children as the holes in a sieve, and even one more, and they had not a scrap of food to eat.

Once the man received a pitcher of milk from a neighbor. He was so hungry that he drank the milk at a gulp, except what he spilled on the table.

Soon a swarm of flies covered the spilled milk. The Gypsy got his makeshift flyswatter and swatted twelve flies with one swat.

"Well," he exclaimed, "what a strong man I am to kill twelve flies in one swat!"

He then got a scrap of paper and a pencil and made a small sign: Twelve at a swat! and stuck it on his forehead.

He said to himself, "If I am so strong, I should go out into the world to seek my fortune. May the whole world see and know how strong I am!"

With this he took to the road. By evening he arrived at a big forest. He saw some light, and as he went closer, he saw a fire. A giant was lying by the fire, but in the eeriness of the dusk the Gypsy thought that it might be a devil with horns. What it was he did not know.

The giant was sound asleep. His snoring was so loud that it put the trees in motion. The Gypsy got a sprig of grass and tickled the giant's nose. That made him sneeze so powerfully that the branches of some trees broke off. It also awakened the giant.

Looking around and seeing the Gypsy, the giant asked, "Who are you, and what brings you here?"

"I was forced to stop here by your powerful sneezing," said the Gypsy. "You see that even the branches of the trees came crashing down around my head. I am lucky just to be alive."

"I see that you have some writing on your forehead," said the giant. "Come closer to the fire so that I can read it."

The Gypsy complied, and when the giant read the sign, he asked, " Are you really so strong?"

"Yes, I am as strong as the sign says," replied the Gypsy.

"Then let's have a contest of strength," said the giant.

At that he got out a club that was so heavy the Gypsy could not lift it.

"Come, let's see which one of us can throw this the highest into the sky," said the giant. At once he threw the club so high that it took three days for it to come down. When it was the Gypsy's turn, he kept looking up into the sky, all the while wondering how to throw the club.

"Why are you looking into the sky?" asked the giant.

"My older brother is up there, and if I throw this club up to him, I am sure that he will drop it down right on your head," answered the Gypsy.

"Then it is better for you to leave the club where it is," said the giant. "If it were to fall on my head, it would be the end of me. I will just accept that you are as strong as the sign says."

That time the Gypsy escaped—for the moment.

Then the giant said, "Come on; I will take you home to my mother. I would like for her to see how strong you are."

"I will go with you," said the Gypsy, "but you will have to carry me, because I don't know the way."

The giant put him on one shoulder and carried him home.

There he called to his mother and said, "Look, mother dear. I have brought a man who is stronger than I."

She was surprised to hear such a thing and asked, "How can a Gypsy be stronger than a giant?"

"We will test him, and you will see. I tested him in the forest, and he was ready to throw my club up to his brother in heaven," said the giant.

After a time the giant had decided on the test. He suggested to the Gypsy, "We will both get pitchforks and take our stand outside by the hedge. Whoever can jab the other first is the winner."

Once in their places the giant somehow got entangled in the hedge. The Gypsy took advantage of the situation and punched the giant as full of holes as one pricks a potato for baking.

Back home the bleeding giant said, "Look, mother dear. He won the contest. Isn't he a strong fellow?"

The mother then prepared a good meal for the Gypsy and sent him off to bed.

When they thought that he was asleep, she said, "My dear son, you had better kill that Gypsy or he will humiliate you again and again."

"Yes, dear mother," he said. "In the middle of the night when he is sound asleep, I will kill him with my iron club."

The Gypsy, who was not asleep, heard all this. He got out of bed, got a log, put it under the covers, and placed his fur cap on it. Then he hid under the bed.

At midnight the giant fetched his iron club and, going quietly to the bed, struck the place where the Gypsy's head would have been with all his might.

From under the bed the Gypsy said softly, "Don't stroke my head so gently."

Terrified, the giant went and told his mother, "I struck his head with all my might, and he asked me not to stroke his head so gently. What a strong man he must really be!"

"Then you must take him back home. Otherwise we will never be rid of him," advised the mother.

Sure that he was safe for the rest of the night, the Gypsy quietly removed the log from the bed and crawled in. All was quiet until the morning.

At breakfast the giants were unusually kind to him. The mother said, "It is time for you to go home. Here is a bag of gold coins. Now leave."

"Dear woman," said the Gypsy, "I came here on your son's shoulder and I do not know the way home. If you want me to go home, your son will have to take me there."

The giant hoisted him and the bag of gold coins to his shoulder and left for the Gypsy village. When they arrived, many Gypsy children ran out to meet them and talked excitedly in their Romany language. The giant did not understand a word.

"What are they talking about?" asked the giant.

"They asked me if I brought home only one giant. They are very hungry, and one giant like you will not be enough to feed them," said the Gypsy.

Terrified that the Gypsy might kill him on the spot and feed him to the children, the giant hastily put the Gypsy and his bag of gold coins on the ground and fled. He has never been seen there again.

From that time on the Gypsy had enough money to feed his children, and he never needed to receive another pitcher of milk from his neighbor.

The Rom—popularly called Gypsies— settled in Hungary during the reign of King Sigismund of Luxemburg (1387–1437). A nomadic people originally from India, the Gypsies had spread into Europe in the fifteenth century. Their skills as weapon-forgers and musicians enabled them to integrate into society. Those without skills lived in shanty towns and in great poverty, and many lived by their wits.

Over the years Hungarian Gypsy violinists and composers became known far and wide. Czinka Panna, the Gypsy girl violinist, accompanied Rákóczi Ferenc II and his freedom fighters in the battles against the Hapsburg oppressors in the early eighteenth century. Later her "Rákóczi Marching Song" inspired the great French composer Berlioz in his work.

The art of the Hungarian Gypsy musicians has enjoyed the recognition of great composers and performers such as Franz Liszt, Franz Erkel, Brahms, Richard Strauss, Delibes, and Yehudi Menuhin.

THE THREE WANDERERS

O*nce upon a time,* long ago, three quick-witted wanderers met somewhere. They had everything a man could need except for one: Money.

One man, especially, needed money. His very ill mother had already sold her small home to pay for doctors, medicine, and transportation. He encouraged the others to rack their brains for an idea of how to get money—lots of it, if possible.

One of them thought of an idea and said, "In this area there is no one so greedy and rich as the ferryman. My mother has often complained about him. My idea is to call myself St. Peter and the two of you will be St. Paul and St. John. If necessary, I will sell my boots and cloak to buy a large fish, a large loaf of bread, and a jug of good wine for our purposes. Then leave the rest to me!"

No sooner said than done!

On their way to the river, they bought a large fish from a

poor fisherman who was grateful for the business, a large loaf of bread from a baker, and a jug of fine wine from an innkeeper. They were almost ready. They lacked only the proper clothes.

At a church they borrowed a priestly robe for St. Peter and two white shirts, one each for the other two not-so-saintly saints. Now they were ready for their mission.

Soon they were at the home of the ferryman. St. Peter knocked at the door, and they were politely admitted. St. Peter took up his station in the entryway with their provisions, St. Paul at the door, and St. John in the kitchen.

"Who are you?" asked the ferryman's wife. "Why have you come here and why are you standing where you are?"

"I am St. Peter," said the oldest wanderer, all dressed in his priestly robe. "My companions are St. Paul and St. John."

"Oh, my God!" exclaimed the woman. "What have we done to deserve a visit from three distinguished guests from the beyond?"

Her husband could say nothing.

Wanting to show hospitality to their guests, she and her husband disappeared into the kitchen to prepare some food. From his abundant supply, the ferryman fetched his smallest fish for his wife to prepare.

St. John, however, saw the man's stinginess. He took the fish in his hands and said, "First I must take it to St. Paul and St. Peter for them to bless it." He rushed to the entry.

Leaving the small fish with his companions, St. John returned to the kitchen with the large fish bought from the poor fisherman. Thinking that St. Peter and St. Paul had performed a miracle, the ferryman and his wife gazed at the fish in astonishment.

"Here, prepare this," said St. John. "It is large enough to feed five people well. Have you any bread for us to eat with the fish?"

The man went into the pantry and brought out his smallest loaf of dry, black bread. He was still as stingy as ever.

St. John took the bread in his hand and said, "First I must take it to St. Paul and St. Peter for them to bless it."

Leaving the small loaf with them, St. John returned to the kitchen with the large loaf of fresh bread bought from the baker. Again, the ferryman and his wife stared open-mouthed. Two miracles were almost too much to believe.

"Here, serve this with the fish," he said. "It is large enough to feed five people well. Have you anything for us to drink when we eat the fish and bread?"

The ferryman returned once more to the pantry. Still stingy, he fetched a small bottle of wine vinegar.

St. John took the small bottle in his hand and said, "First I must take it to St. Paul and St. Peter for them to bless it."

Leaving it with them, St. John returned to the kitchen with the jug of good wine bought from the innkeeper. "Here," he said, "let's drink this with our fish and bread. It is enough for five people."

By then the greedy couple believed they had seen miracles. The wife whispered to her husband, "What do you think of their blessing a sack of our gold?"

"Ah," said her husband, "that is exactly what I was thinking."

Excusing herself and disappearing into an adjoining room, the woman took out a sack of gold coins from its hiding place. Soon she returned and asked St. John to bless their sack of gold.

Everything was working according to plan.

St. John said, "I will take it to St. Paul and St. Peter for them to bless it."

St. Paul was still at his station at the door. He took the bag of gold coins and ran out as fast as he could with it. St. Peter disappeared right behind him.

The couple was getting impatient. "Why is it taking so long this time?" they asked St. John, who had returned to the kitchen.

"Gold is harder than fish, bread, and wine," he said. "I will go to learn how much longer they think it will take. Perhaps with my blessing the gold can be multiplied even more."

With this, he, too, disappeared, leaving the couple waiting in the kitchen. Soon their impatience sent them to the entryway. They saw nothing and no one.

"They have returned beyond the pearly gates with our gold!" the wife exclaimed.

Realizing he had been tricked, the ferryman wailed in grief.

Hungary is cut through by two important rivers, the Danube and the Tisza. Before bridges crossed them, ferryboats carried people and goods

across and the person who operated the boat was the ferryman. Ferry-
boat landings at border crossings on the Danube and Tisza also served as
customs posts. The ferrymen received the transportation fee, and the customs officials received the duty and often became rich by accepting bribes
for tariff reduction. Ferrymen involved in that corrupt system became rich,
as did the ferryman in this tale.

Lookout Mountain, or, The Legend of the Chimney-Stack Cake

When the Tatars invaded Transylvania, the Szekler watchmen ignited their watch fires and stormbells tolled everywhere: "The Tatars are coming!"

The bells were ringing at Máréfalva, and the village mayor alerted all the inhabitants. He sent watchmen up to the peak of Lookout Mountain to guard and to look for any warnings sent from Budvár near Udvarhely. He hid the women and children in a cave in the mountain and filled it with supplies.

Soon the watchmen came running and shouting, "The Tatars are here!"

The mayor led the fighting men into another well-supplied cave, from which they could shoot their arrows at the invaders.

The Tatars entered the village with a loud war cry. They looked for people in houses and in the church, but they found none. Then they found the trail that led to the caves. Once at the base of the mountain, they began their climb.

The mayor and four men fortified the entrance to the cave and shot their arrows at the invaders. But they could see that their arrows were nearly useless against such a horde. The mayor took direct aim at the Tatar khan, who fell dead from his horse with an arrow through his heart.

At this the horde became terrified and withdrew to a safer distance. They settled in the valley and the slow siege began. They expected the Szeklers to eventually starve to death.

After a time their food supplies began to dwindle. Yet no one could leave the caves, because the Tatars seemed to have a thousand eyes. The only communication between the two caves was through a speaker-funnel.

Through this the mayor said to his wife, "We will break out and fight, because it is a disgrace for a soldier to starve to death."

"You don't need to do that, my good husband," replied his wife. "I have a plan that will drive away the Tatars."

The skillful woman braided straw in the shape of a chimney-stack cake. Then she stuck it on a pole and placed it in the sight of the Tatars below. "Look," she shouted. "You are starving to death while we are eating like royalty. How long will you be such fools?"

The Tatars, without their khan to lead them, became angry at the thought that the Szeklers were eating delicacies while they were barely existing. They entered the village, pillaged it, and burned it to the ground. Thinking that they had everything to lose and nothing to gain, they withdrew from Máré-falva and went on their way.

When it was safe, the Szeklers returned to the site of their village and rebuilt it.

To this day the traditional Szekler cake is the *kürtős kalács*. The cake has the shape of a chimney-stack but not its size.

The half-nomadic Tatar tribes with their reputation for savagery swarmed over the territory of the Ukraine and captured its capital city, Kiev, in 1240. In the spring of 1241 under Batu Khan, the Tatars descended to the fields before the Carpathian Mountains, often referred to as the Transylvanian Alps. It was particularly Transylvania and its Szeklers that suffered greatly from the raids of these Mongol forces. Over the centuries the Szeklers had the noble task of guarding the frontiers of European civilization from the dangerous storms of Asian invaders. The Tatar empire disintegrated in the fifteenth century.

THE LEGEND OF THE WHITE STAG

T*wo generations after* the Flood, recorded in Jewish sacred literature, lived the mighty prince, Ménrót, grandson of Noah. From the mountains of Ararat in the area of ancient Urartu, Ménrót's father, Japheth, migrated toward Persia. Because of his passion for hunting, Ménrót settled there amidst such an abundance of game.

As stories go, the handsome Ménrót married the beautiful Persian woman Enéh, who bore him two sons, Hunor and Magor, the mighty warriors who became the fathers of the Huns and the Magyars, today known as Hungarians.

Driven by his passion for hunting, Ménrót got up every morning, took care of his daily affairs, mounted his stallion with bow and quiver in hand, and left for the hunt. His quarry was usually a bird. At full gallop he could bring down any bird. Once he targeted it, it was as good as dead.

Although he liked to hunt alone, when Hunor and Magor

were old enough, he took them with him. At their father's side, they, too, learned to shoot birds at full gallop.

Seeing that they had become as skilled as he, Ménrót was very proud. He used to say, "My sons may become better hunters than I."

The boys became strong and handsome young men. Ménrót knew it was time for them to leave the family tent and to have their own. He said, "My sons, I am old and no longer able to go hunting with you. You are well prepared to make your way in life. Now I will give you land, forests, servants, horses, and livestock. After I close my eyes for the last time, you will be the rulers of this land. Be wise and take good care of it, and it will take good care of you."

Hunor and Magor were sad, but they knew that their father was right. They thanked him for his generosity, and the next day built tents at some distance on the top of a beautiful hill, where they settled with their servants and livestock.

In the beginning, they hunted in the forests near their tents, but little by little they ventured farther and farther. Still, by evening they returned home and reported to their old father where they had been, the game they had taken and how many times they missed the target.

One evening while sitting around the fire, Hunor said to Magor: "My brother, I have an idea. Let's leave tomorrow morning on a longer hunting trip. Let's see what's beyond our borders. Is the game more abundant? Are the rivers bigger? Do they have more fish in them? It will do us no harm to see."

"I, too, have thought about such a trip," said Magor. "Here we know every bush, nook, and cranny of field and forest. We know the buffalo, bears, stags, eagles, falcons, and all other birds of the air. Their number is steadily decreasing because of our hunting."

They agreed to leave at daybreak to go west. Each selected from his men fifty of the best hunters and prepared provisions.

By daybreak Hunor and Magor, together with their men, were riding and hunting. When evening came, they pitched their tents, made a fire, and spent the night in the camp. The next day they continued westward, hunting as they rode.

After some days the party crossed the borders of their country. The farther they went, the more they liked the forests and fields. Crossing vast areas, they found themselves again and again in lush forests teeming with game.

They hunted to their hearts' content. Hunor and Magor thought often about their father and wished him beside them. They found buffalo and deer grazing in every clearing. Yet they preferred the hunt to the kill. They often chased a single animal through the forest from morning until evening.

One day the brothers caught sight of a white stag of magnificent beauty. They had never seen such an animal before. His antlers were like a crown on his head, and his eyes were like black diamonds. His waist was slender and supple, and his thin but strong legs seemed to glide rather than to run.

"Look, Brother!" shouted Hunor.

"Amazing, marvelous," exclaimed Magor. "Go! Go!"

The stag ran with lightning speed, and the brothers with their men raced after him. The stag lured them from clearing to dense forest and over mountains and through ravines. Although the horses were tiring, Hunor and Magor spurred them on, continuing the chase. They wanted to capture the stag and take him to their father. At about sunset the stag disappeared in a dense, reedy swamp. The chase ended.

In the morning light the brothers realized that they were in a beautiful land. Before them were a peninsula, forests, and a vast lake. Hunor and Magor walked amidst a profusion of flowers. Large trees shaded them and provided fruit and the waters were teeming with fish.

"How I would like to remain here forever!" said Hunor. "What about you, Brother?"

"I, too, would like it, but what will our father think? To-morrow we must leave for home."

On their way they hunted only as much as necessary for their daily food. The journey lasted seven days and seven nights. Only then did they realize how far they had been from home.

When Hunor and Magor arrived, they found their father lying in his tent, unable to get up. He was sad and spoke softly, "Where were you? I have not seen you for two times seven days and nights. I feel that my end is near."

"Forgive us, Father, that our passion for hunting drove us too far," said Hunor. "Now we have returned to tell you that we found a beautiful country where both of us would like to settle."

"Isn't my country good enough for you?" asked their father.

"Father, you have other sons. Let them have this land. Please give us your blessing and let us go where the hunting and fishing are as we have never before seen in our lives."

With tear-filled eyes Ménrót said, "Come and kneel before me that I may bless you."

Hunor and Magor knelt, and their father said: "Go, and may God direct you. May blessing and good fortune follow you wherever you go."

Kissing his two sons, Ménrót breathed his last. On the morrow all his sons buried him with the dignity due a prince.

Having done their duty to their father, Hunor and Magor prepared for the journey. This time they took their hundred men, servants, and livestock. As before, they traveled seven days and seven nights. When they arrived, they knelt down, thanked God for their new homeland, and praised the white stag that had lured them there.

The origin and kinship of Hungarians are hotly debated issues. According to Kézai Simon's chronicle, *Gesta Hungarorum*, written in 1283, Hunor and Magor followed the trail of the white stag into the Maeotian marshes near ancient Persia. Apart from a narrow wading place this region is enclosed by the Sea of Azov. Access to and exit from it are difficult. Once in the Maeotian marshes, Hunor and Magor did not move for five years. In the sixth year they ventured out to the land of the Alans, situated in North Caucasus, who led the warring lifestyle of the nomads. Hunor and Magor found only women and children whose menfolk had gone to war. Here they seized the two daughters of Dula, the prince of the Alans, for their brides. All the Huns descend from these women. Because the small land of Maeotis could not support their growing number, Hunor and Magor moved on with all their people and occupied the territory from the Volga River to the Caucasus Mountains. Their descendants settled along the River Volga in an area known as Magna Hungaria, now Bashkiria in the South Ural Mountains. In a protracted scramble for living space, the Hungarians were pushed westward by their powerful enemies, the Petchenegs, to Etelköz, directly in the lee of the Carpathians. Their migrations lasted more than four centuries and ended in what is now Hungary.

"The Legend of the White Stag" is one of several stories dealing with the origin of Hungarians. Perhaps someday the riddle will be solved. Until then the jury will remain out, and we will await its verdict.

BIBLIOGRAPHY

In Hungarian the last name is given first and then the first name follows.

BOOKS

Bálint, Csaba. *Hétszázhetvenhét Magyar Népmese.* Budapest: Videopont Kiadó, 1995.

Bárczi, Géza. *A Magyar Nyelv Életrajza.* Budapest: Gondolat Kiadó, 1963.

Berze Nagy, János. *Magyar Népmesetípusok.* Pécs, Hungary: Baranya Megye Tanácsának Kiadása, 1957.

Benedek, Elek. *Többsincs Királyfi és Más Mesék.* Budapest: Móra Ferenc Kiadó, 1975.

Benedek, Elek. *A Százesztendős Jövendőmondó.* Bukarest: Irodalmi Könyvkiadó, 1967.

Illyés, Gyula. *Hetvenhét Magyar Népmese.* Budapest: Móra Ferenc Könyvkiadó, 1993.

Jankovics, Marcell. *Ahol a Madár se Jár.* Budapest: Pontifex Kiadó, 1996.

Kriza, János. *Vadrózsák.* Bukarest: Kriterion Könyvkiadó, 1975.

Lázár, István. *Hungary, a Brief History.* Budapest: Corvina Books, 1996.

Lengyel, Dénes. *Régi Magyar Mondák.* Budapest: Móra Ferenc Kiadó, 1996.

Megyesy, Jenő. *Szállj Nóta, Szállj.* Tulsa, Oklahoma: PVH Publishing Inc., 1997.

Molnár, Irma. *Old Székely Cuisine.* Unpublished.

Orbán, Balázs. *A Székelyföld.* Budapest: Europa Könyvkiadó, 1982.

Ortutay, Gyula. *Magyar Néprajzi Lexikon.* Budapest: Akadémiai Kiadó, 1980.

Palkó, Zsuzsanna and Linda Dégh. *Hungarian Folktales: The Art of Zsuzsanna Palkó.* Translated by Vera Kalm. Jackson: University Press of Mississippi, 1995.

Romsics, Ignác. *Magyarország Története a XX. Században.* Budapest: Osiris Kiadó, 1999.

Rónai, András. *Térképezett Történelem.* Budapest: Püski Kiadó, 1993.

Sebestyén, Ádám. *Bukovinai Székely Népmesék.* Szekszárd, Hungary: Tolna Megyei Tanács, 1979.

Szép, Ernő. *Mátyás Király Tréfái.* Budapest: Móra Ferenc Kiadó, 1994.

Unger, Mátyás, and Szabolcs, Ottó. *Magyarország Története.* Budapest: Gondolat Kiadó, 1965.

ADDITIONAL RESOURCES

Hungarian Electronic Library: http://www.mek.iif.hu/

Szathmáry Archives. Louis Szathmáry Family Collection of
Hungarica, The University of Chicago Library, Illinois.